Dressing Up for the Carnival

Carol Shields's novels include *Larry's Party* (1997), winner of the 1998 Orange Prize; *The Stone Diaries* (1993), winner of the Pulitzer Prize and shortlisted for the Booker Prize; *The Republic of Love* (1992); *Happenstance* (1991) and *Mary Swann* (1990). *Various Miracles*, a collection of short stories, was published in 1994. Born and brought up in Chicago, Carol Shields has lived in Canada since 1957. She is the Chancellor of the University of Winnipeg.

'Shields has the master's touch of painting the broader picture and illuminating with minute detail; she writes as easily about men as about women, seamlessly changing tense and tempo, tone and scale. Her narrative voice is at once cosy and impressive, intimate and authoritative. In her hands, the reader has a sense of security and immense pleasure. Who could ask for more?' *Daily Mail*

'Carol Shields uses language as a great chef uses pastry. In her hands it is light, delicate, and forms elaborately perfect structures. These witty, sensitive stories feature the brave, the resolute, the affectionate, the tolerant, the lonely and the free. The whole confection is delicious.' *Harpers & Queen*

'Each sentence has been fashioned with care. The balance, texture and structure matter to the writer as much as balance, texture and structure matter to individual lives. Nature and domesticity is a deceptive collusion, concealing seams of passion, anger, regret and the frankly weird, and its fractures have been transcribed on to the page by a watcher with brilliant powers of observation. This is a collection to be luxuriously savoured.' *The Times*

'These stories, in their variety, in the elegance of the prose – "with sentences that melted at the centre and branched at the ends", as she puts it in one of them – with their optimism and unexpected puzzles leave the reader with a sense of admiration.' *Spectator*

'Whether she deflates pretensions with a cunning wit, or reveals the complex depths of feeling that ennoble humans, Shields is as wise and sympathetic as ever.' *Woman's Journal*

'Each tale has its own distinct flavour. Shields is generous with her ingredients, flinging in with a profligate hand insights, ideas and phrases which a meaner, less inspired person might have saved for presentation as the *pièce de résistance* of a banquet, and the book is scattered with delicious morsels, "an owl hooting its signature on the night sky", "question marks hovering over words like a jangle of surprised coat hangers". Read this book. *Bon appétit*.' *Sunday Express*

'Reading Carold Shields is like drinking a zestful glass of home-made lemonade on a hot and sleepy afternoon.' *Evening Standard*

'In a collection that is remarkably easy on the eye, wry and analytical about differences between men and women, and emphatic and generous in the familiarity of its tone, Shields continues her quiet, impactful chronicling of the modern. She is one of the most determinedly long-sighted of our writers, putting her trust, as one of her characters says, "in the simplifying afterlight of metaphor, which is all we have."' *Scotsman*

Dressing Up
for the Carnival

—

Carol Shields

FOURTH ESTATE • *London*

For Evan, Eli, and Rebecca

This paperback edition first published 2000
First published in Great Britain in 2000 by
Fourth Estate Limited
6 Salem Road
London W2 4BU
www.4thestate.co.uk

Some of the stories in this collection have appeared previously in the UK:
'Mirrors' in *Good Housekeeping* 1996 and the *Daily Telegraph* 1999; 'Our Men
and Women' in *W Magazine* 1996; 'New Music' in *BBC Music Magazine* 1999;
'Soup du Jour' in *Woman and Home* 1996; 'The Next Best Kiss' in *Prospect*
1999; 'A Scarf' in *Sunday Express Magazine* 2000; 'Dressing Down' in
Woman and Home 2000.

1 3 5 7 9 10 8 6 4 2

ISBN 1-84115-402-4

Typeset by Rowland Phototypesetting Ltd,
Bury St Edmunds, Suffolk
Printed in Great Britain by
Cox & Wyman, Reading, Berks

CONTENTS

Dressing Up
for the Carnival

—

ALL OVER TOWN people are putting on their costumes. Tamara has flung open her closet door; just to see her standing there is to feel a squeeze of the heart. She loves her clothes. She *knows* her clothes. Her favourite moment of the day is *this* moment, standing at the closet door, still a little dizzy from her long night of tumbled sleep, biting her lip, thinking hard, moving the busy hangers along the rod, about to make up her mind.

Yes! The yellow cotton skirt with the big patch pockets and the hand detail around the hem. How fortunate to own such a skirt. And the white blouse. What a blouse! Those sleeves, that neckline with its buttoned flap, the fullness in the yoke that reminds her of the Morris dances she and her boyfriend Bruce saw at the Exhibition last year.

Next she adds her new straw belt; perfect. A string of yellow beads. Earrings of course. Her bone sandals. And bare legs, why not?

She never checks the weather before she dresses; her clothes *are* the weather, as powerful in their sunniness as the strong, muzzy early morning light pouring into the narrow street by the bus stop, warming the combed crown of her hair and fuelling her with imagination. She taps a sandalled foot lightly on the pavement, waiting for the number 4 bus, no longer just Tamara, clerk-receptionist for the Youth Employment Bureau, but a woman in a yellow skirt. A passionate woman dressed in yellow. A Passionate, Vibrant Woman About To Begin Her Day. Her Life.

Roger, aged thirty, employed by the Gas Board, is coming out of a corner grocer's carrying a mango in his left hand. He went in to buy an apple and came out with *this*. At the cash register he refused a bag, preferring to carry this thing, this object, in his bare hand. The price was $1.29. He's a little surprised at how heavy it is, a tight seamless leather skin enclosing soft pulp, or so he imagines. He has never bought a mango before, never eaten one, doesn't know what a mango tastes like or how it's prepared. Cooked like a squash? Sliced and sugared like a peach? He has no intention of eating it, not now anyway, maybe never. Its weight reminds him of a first-class league ball, but larger, longer, smooth skinned, and ripely green. Mango, mango. An elliptical purse, juice-filled, curved for the palm of the human hand, his hand.

He is a man of medium height, burly, divorced, wearing an open-necked shirt, hurrying back to work after his coffee break. But at this moment he freezes and sees himself freshly: a man carrying a mango in his left hand. Already he's accustomed to it; in fact, it's starting to feel lighter and drier, like a set of castanets which has somehow attached itself to his left arm. Any minute now he'll break out into a cha-cha-cha right here in front of the Gas Board. The shrivelled fate he sometimes sees for himself can be postponed if only he puts his mind to it. Who would have thought it of him? Not his ex-wife Lucile, not his co-workers, not his boss, not even himself.

And the Borden sisters are back from their ski week in Happy Valley. They've been back for a month now, in fact, so why are they still wearing those little plastic ski passes on the zipper tabs of their jackets? A good question. I SKIED HAPPY MOUNTAIN these passes say. The Bordens wear them all over town, at the shopping centre, in the parking lot. It's spring, the leaves are unfolding on the hedges in front of the post office, but the Borden girls, Karen and Sue, still carry on their bodies, and in their faces too, the fresh wintry cold of the slopes, the thrill of powder snow and stinging sky. (The air up there chimes with echoes, a bromide of blue.) It would be an exaggeration to say the Borden sisters swagger; it would be going too far. They move like young ponies, quivery and thoughtful, with the memory of expended effort and banked curves. They speak to each other in voices that are loud and musical, and their skin, so clear, pink, bright, and healthy, traps the sunshine beneath its surface. With one hand, walking along, they stroke the feathering–out tops of hedges in front of the post office, and with the other they pull and tug on those little plasticized tags—I SKIED HAPPY MOUNTAIN. You might say it's a kind of compulsion, as though they can't help themselves.

And then there's Wanda from the bank who has been sent on the strangest of errands. It happened in this way: Mr. Wishcourt, the bank manager where Wanda works, has just bought a new baby carriage for his wife, or rather, for their new baby son, Samuel James. The baby carriage was an impulsive lunch-hour purchase, he explains to Wanda, looking shamefaced but exuberant: an English pram, high-wheeled, majestically hooded, tires like a Rolls-Royce, a beauty, but the fool thing, even when folded up, refuses to fit in the back of his Volvo. Would she object? It would take perhaps three-quarters of an hour. It's a fine day. He'll draw her a plan on a sheet of paper, put an X where his house is. He knows how she loves walking, that she gets restless in the afternoon sometimes, sitting in her little airless cage. He would appreciate it so much. And so would his wife and little Sam. Would she mind? He's never before asked her to make coffee or do personal errands. It's against his policy, treating his employees like that. But just this once?

Wanda sets off awkwardly. She is, after all, an awkward woman, who was formerly an awkward girl with big girlish teeth and clumsy shoulders. The pram's swaying body seems to steer her at first, instead of *her* steering *it*. Such a chunky rolling oblong, black and British with its wambling, bossy, outsized keel. "Excuse me," she says, and "Sorry." Without meaning to, she forces people over to the edge of the sidewalks, crowds them at the street corners, even rubs up against them with the big soft tires.

All she gets back are smiles. Or kindly little nods that say: "It's not your fault" or "How marvellous" or "What a picture!" After a bit she gets the hang of steering. This is a technical marvel she's pushing along, the way it takes the curbs, soundlessly with scarcely any effort at all. Engineering at its most refined and comical. Her hands rest lightly on the wide white handlebar. It might be made of ivory or alabaster or something equally precious, it's so smooth and cool to the touch.

By the time Wanda reaches Pine Street she feels herself fully in charge. Beneath the leafy poplars, she and the carriage have become a single entity. Gliding, melding, a silvery hum of wheels and a faint, pleasing adhesive resistance as the tires roll along suburban asphalt. The weight of her fingertips is enough to keep it in motion, in control, and she takes the final corners with grace. Little Sam is going to love his new rolling home, so roomy and rhythmic, like a dark boat sailing forward in tune with his infant breathing and the bump-dee-bump of his baby heart.

She stops, leans over, and reaches inside. There's no one about; no one sees her, only the eyes inside her head that have rehearsed this small gesture in dreams. She straightens the blanket, pulling it smooth, pats it into place. "Shhh," she murmurs, smiling. "There, there, now."

Mr. Gilman is smiling too. His daughter-in-law, who considers him a prehistoric bore, has invited him to dinner. This happens perhaps once a month; the telephone rings early in the morning. "We'd love to have you over tonight," she says. "Just family fare, I'm afraid, leftovers."

"I'd be delighted," he always says, even though the word *leftovers* gives him, every time she says it, a little ping of injury.

At age eighty he can be observed in his obverse infancy, metaphorically sucking and tonguing the missing tooth of his life. He knows what he looks like: the mirror tells all— eyes like water sacs, crimson arcs around the ears, a chin that betrays him, the way it mooches and wobbles while he thrashes around in his head for one of those rumpled anecdotes that seem only to madden his daughter-in-law. Better to keep still and chew. "Scrumptious," he always says, hoping to win her inhospitable heart, but knowing he can't.

Today he decides to buy her flowers. Why-oh-why has

he never thought of this before! Daffodils are selling for $1.99 a half dozen. A bargain. It must be spring, he thinks, looking around. Why not buy two bunches, or three? Why not indeed? Or four?

They form a blaze of yellow in his arms, a sweet propitiating little fire. He knows he should take them home immediately and put them in water for tonight, but he's reluctant to remove the green paper wrapping which lends a certain legitimacy; these aren't flowers randomly snatched from the garden; these are florist's flowers, purchased as an offering, an oblation.

There seems nothing to do but carry them about with him all day. He takes them along to the bank, the drugstore, to his appointment with the foot specialist, his afternoon card club at the Sunset Lodge. Never has he received more courteous attention, such quick service. The eyes of strangers appear friendlier than usual. "I am no worse off than the average person," he announces to himself. He loses, gracefully, at canasta, then gets a seat on the bus, a seat by the window. The pale flowers in his arms spell evanescence, gaiety. "Hello there," a number of people call out to him. He is clearly a man who is expected somewhere, anticipated. A charming gent, elegant and dapper, propounding serious questions, bearing gifts, flowers. A man in disguise.

Ralph Eliot, seventeen years old, six feet tall, killingly handsome, and the best halfback the school team has seen in years, has carelessly left his football helmet hanging on a hook on the back of his bedroom door. An emergency of the first order; his ten-year-old sister Mandy is summoned to bring it to the playing field.

She runs all the way up Second Avenue; at the traffic light she strikes a pose, panting, then pounds furiously the whole length of Sargent Street, making it in four minutes flat. She carries the helmet by its tough plastic chin strap and as she runs along, it bangs against her bare leg. She feels her breath blazing into a spray of heroic pain, and as her foot rounds on the pavement a filament of recognition is touched. The exactitude of the gesture doubles and divides inside her head, and for the first time she comprehends *who* her brother is, that deep-voiced stranger whose bedroom is next to her own. Today, for a minute, she *is* her brother. *She* is Ralph Eliot, age seventeen, six feet tall, who later this afternoon will make a dazzling, lazy touchdown, bringing reward and honour to his name, and hers.

Susan Gourley, first-year arts student, has been assigned Beckett's *Waiting for Godot*. She carries it under her arm so that the title is plainly visible. She is a girl with a look of lustreless inattention and a reputation for drowsiness, but she's always known this to be a false assessment. She's biding her time, waiting; today she strides along, *strides*, her book flashing under her arm. She is a young woman who is reading a great classic. Vistas of possibility unfold like money.

Molly Beale's briny old body has been propelled downtown by her cheerful new pacemaker, and there she bumps into Bert Lessing, the city councillor, whose navy blue beret, complete with military insignia, rides pertly over his left ear. They converse like lovers. They bristle with wit. They chitter like birds.

Jeanette Foster is sporting a smart chignon. Who does she think she *is*! Who *does* she think she is?

A young woman, recently arrived in town and rather lonely, carries her sandwiches to work in an old violin case. This is only temporary. Tomorrow she may use an ordinary paper bag or eat in the cafeteria.

We cannot live without our illusions, thinks X, an anonymous middle-aged citizen who, sometimes, in the privacy of his own bedroom, in the embrace of happiness, waltzes about in his wife's lace-trimmed nightgown. His wife is at bingo, not expected home for an hour. He lifts the blind an inch and sees the sun setting boldly behind his pear tree, its mingled coarseness and refinement giving an air of confusion. Everywhere he looks he observes cycles of consolation and enhancement, and now it seems as though the evening itself is about to alter its dimensions, becoming more (and also less) than what it really is.

A Scarf

TWO YEARS AGO I wrote a novel, and my publisher sent me on a three-city book tour: New York, Washington, and Baltimore. A very modest bit of promotion, you might say, but Scribano & Lawrence scarcely knew what to do with me. I had never written a novel before. I am a middle-aged woman, not at all remarkable-looking and certainly not media-smart. If I have any reputation at all it is for being an editor and scholar, and not for producing, to everyone's amazement, a "fresh, bright, springtime piece of fiction," or so it was described in *Publishers Weekly*.

My Thyme Is Up baffled everyone with its sparky sales. We had no idea who was buying it; I didn't know and Mr. Scribano didn't know. "Probably young working girls," he ventured, "gnawed by loneliness and insecurity."

These words hurt my feelings slightly, but then the

reviews, good as they were, had subtly injured me too. The reviewers seemed taken aback that my slim novel (200 pages exactly) possessed any weight at all. "Oddly appealing," the *New York Times Book Review* said. "Mrs. Winters' book is very much for the moment, though certainly not for the ages," the *New Yorker* said. My husband Tom advised me to take this as praise, his position being that all worthy novels pay close attention to the time in which they are suspended, and sometimes, years later, despite themselves, acquire a permanent lustre. I wasn't so sure. As a long-time editor of Danielle Westerman's work, I had acquired a near-crippling degree of critical appreciation for the sincerity of her moral stance, and I understood perfectly well that there was something just a little bit *darling* about my own book.

My three daughters, Nancy, Chris, and Norah, all teenagers, were happy about the book because they were mentioned by name in a *People* magazine interview. ("Mrs. Winters lives on a farm outside Lancaster, Pennsylvania, is married to a family physician, and is the mother of three handsome daughters, Nancy, Christine, and Norah.") That was enough for them. Handsome. Norah, the most literary of the three—both Nancy and Chris are in the advanced science classes at General MacArthur High School —mumbled that it might have been a better book if I'd skipped the happy ending, if Alicia had decided on suicide after all, and if Roman had denied her his affection. There was, my daughters postulated, maybe too much over-the-top sweetness about the thyme seeds Alicia planted in her window-box, with Alicia's mood listless but squeaking hope. And no one in her right mind would sing out (as Alicia had done) those words that reached Roman's ears—he was making filtered coffee in the kitchen—and bound him to her forever: "My thyme is up."

It won the Offenden Prize, which, though the money was nice, shackled the book to minor status. Clarence and Dorothy Offenden had established the prize back in the seventies out of a shared exasperation with the opaqueness of the contemporary novel. "The Offenden Prize recognizes literary quality and honours accessibility." These are their criteria. Dorothy and Clarence are a good-hearted couple, and rich, but a little jolly and simple in their judgments, and Dorothy in particular is fond of repeating her recipe for enduring fiction. "A beginning, a middle, and an ending," she likes to say. "Is that too much to ask!"

At the award ceremony in New York she embraced Tom and the girls, and told them how I shone among my peers, those dabblers in convolution and pretension who wrote without holding the reader in the mind, who played games for their own selfish amusement, and who threw a mask of *noir* over every event, whether it was appropriate or not. "It's heaven," she sang into Tom's ear, "to find that sunniness still exists in the world." (Show me your fatwa, Mrs. Winters.)

I don't consider myself a sunny person. In fact, if I

prayed, I would ask every day to be spared from the shame of dumb sunniness. Danielle Westerman has taught me that much, her life, her reflection on that life. Don't hide your dark side from yourself, she always said, it's what keeps us going forward, that pushing away from the unspeakable brilliance. She wrote, of course, amid the shadows of the Holocaust, and no one expected her to struggle free to merriment.

After the New York event, I said good-bye to the family and got on a train and travelled to Washington, staying in a Georgetown hotel which had on its top floor, reserved for me by my publisher, something called the Writer's Suite. A brass plaque on the door announced this astonishing fact. I, the writer in a beige raincoat, Mrs. Reta Winters from Lancaster, entered this doorway with small suitcase in tow and looked around, not daring to imagine what I might find. There was a salon as well as a bedroom, two full baths, a very wide bed, more sofas than I would have time to sit on in my short stay, and a coffee-table consisting of a sheet of glass posed on three immense faux books lying on their sides, stacked one on the other. A large bookshelf held the tomes of the authors who had stayed in the suite. "We like to ask our guests to contribute a copy of their work," the desk clerk had told me, and I was obliged to explain that I had only a single reading copy with me, but that I would attempt to find a copy in a local store. "That would be most appreciated," she almost whistled into the sleeve of my raincoat.

The books left behind by previous authors were disappointing, inspiration manifestos or self-help manuals, with a few thrillers thrown in. I'm certainly not a snob—I read the Jackie Onassis biography, for example—but my close association with writers such as Danielle Westerman has conditioned me to hope for a degree of ambiguity or nuance and there was none here.

In that great, wide bed I had a disturbing but not unfamiliar dream—it is the dream I always have when I am away from Lancaster, away from the family. I am standing in the kitchen at home, producing a complicated meal for guests, but there is not enough food to work with. In the fridge sits a single egg and maybe a tomato. How am I going to feed all these hungry mouths?

I'm quite aware of how this dream might be analysed by a dream expert, that the scarcity of food stands for a scarcity of love, that no matter how I stretch that egg and tomato, there will never be enough of Reta Winters for everyone who needs her. This is how my friend Gwen, whom I am looking forward to seeing in Baltimore, would be sure to interpret the dream if I were so foolish as to tell her. Gwen is an obsessive keeper of a dream journal—as are quite a number of my friends—and she also records the dreams of others if they are offered and found worthy.

I resist the theory of insufficient love. My dream, I like to think, points only to the abrupt cessation, or interruption, of daily obligation. For twenty years I've been responsible for producing three meals a day for the several individuals I live with. I may not be conscious of this obligation, but surely I must always, at some level, be calculating the amount of food in the house and the number of bodies to be fed; Tom and the girls, the girls' friends, my mother-in-law next door, passing acquaintances. Away from home, liberated from my responsibility for meals, my unexecuted calculations steal into my dreams and leave me blithering with this diminished store of nourishment and the fact of my unpreparedness. Such a small dream crisis, but I always wake with a sense of terror.

Since *My Thyme Is Up* is a first novel and since mine is an unknown name, there was very little for me to do in Washington. Mr. Scribano had been afraid this would happen. The television stations weren't interested, and the radio stations avoided novels unless they had a "topic" like cancer or child abuse.

I managed to fulfill all my obligations in a mere two hours the morning after my arrival, taking a cab to a bookstore called Politics & Prose, where I signed books for three rather baffled-looking customers and then a few more stock copies which the staff was kind enough to produce. I handled the whole thing badly, was overly ebullient with the book buyers, too chatty, wanting them to love me as much as they said they loved my book, wanting them for best friends, you would think. ("Please just call me Reta, everyone does.") My impulse was to apologize for not being younger and more fetching like Alicia in my novel and for not having her bright ingenue voice and manner. I was ashamed of my red pantsuit, catalogue-issue, and wondered if I'd remembered, waking up in the Writer's Suite, to apply deodorant.

From Politics & Prose I took a cab to a store called Pages, where there were no buying customers at all, but where the two young proprietors took me for a splendid lunch at an Italian bistro and also insisted on giving me a free copy of my book to leave in the Writer's Suite. Then it was afternoon, a whole afternoon, and I had nothing to do until the next morning when I was to take my train to Baltimore. Mr. Scribano had warned me I might find touring lonely.

I returned to the hotel, freshened up, and placed my book on the bookshelf. But why had I returned to the hotel? What homing instinct had brought me here when I might be out visiting museums or perhaps taking a tour through the Senate chambers? There was a wide springtime afternoon to fill, and an evening too, since no one had suggested taking me to dinner.

I decided to go shopping in the Georgetown area, having spotted from the taxi a number of tiny boutiques. My daughter Norah's birthday was coming up in a week's time, and she longed to have a beautiful and serious scarf. She had never had a scarf in all her seventeen years, not unless you count the woollen mufflers she wears on the school bus, but since her senior class trip to Paris, she had been talking about the scarves that every chic Frenchwoman wears as part of her wardrobe. These scarves, so artfully draped, were silk, nothing else would do, and their colours shocked and awakened the dreariest of clothes, the wilted navy blazers that Frenchwomen wear or those cheap black cardigans they try to get away with.

I never have time to shop in Lancaster, and, in fact, there would be little available there. But today I had time, plenty of time, and so I put on my low-heeled walking shoes and started out.

Georgetown's boutiques are set amid tiny fronted houses, impeccably gentrified with shuttered bay windows and framed by minuscule gardens, enchanting to the eye. My own sprawling untidy house outside Lancaster, if dropped into this landscape, would destroy half a dozen or more of these meticulous brick facades. The placement of flower-pots was so ardently pursued here, so caring, so solemn, and the clay pots themselves had been rubbed, I could tell, with sandpaper, to give them a country look.

These boutiques held such a minimum of stock that I wondered how they were able to compete with one another. There might be six or seven blouses on a rod, a few cash-mere pullovers, a table casually strewn with shells or stones or Art Nouveau picture frames or racks of antique post-cards. A squadron of very slender saleswomen presided over this spare merchandise, which they fingered in such a loving way that I suddenly wanted to buy everything in sight. The scarves—every shop had a good half dozen—were knotted on dowels, and there was not one that was not pure silk with hand-rolled edges.

I took my time. I realized I would be able, given enough shopping time, to buy Norah the perfect scarf, not the near-perfect and certainly not the impulse purchase we usually settled for at home. She had mentioned wanting something in a bright blue with perhaps some yellow dashes. I would find that very scarf in one of these many boutiques. The thought of myself as a careful and deliberate shopper brought me a bolt of happiness. I took a deep breath and smiled genuinely at the anorexic saleswomen, who seemed to sense and respond to my new consumer eagerness. "That's not quite her," I quickly learned to say, and they nodded with sympathy. Most of them wore scarves themselves around their angular necks, and I admired, to myself, the intricate knotting and colours of these scarves. I admired, too, the women's forthcoming involvement in my mission. "Oh, the scarf absolutely must be suited to the person," they said, or words to that effect—as though they knew Norah personally and understood that she was a young woman of highly defined tastes and requirements which they were anxious to satisfy.

She wasn't really. She is, Tom and I always think, too easily satisfied and someone who too seldom considers herself deserving. When she was a very small child, two or three, eating lunch in her high chair, she heard an airplane go overhead and looked up at me and said, "The pilot doesn't know I'm eating an egg." She seemed shocked at this perception, but willing to register the shock calmly so as not to alarm me. She would be grateful for any scarf I brought her, pleased I had taken the time, but for once I wanted, and had an opportunity to procure, a scarf that would gladden her heart.

As I moved from one boutique to the next I began to form a very definite idea of the scarf I wanted for Norah, and began, too, to see how impossible it might be to accomplish this task. The scarf became an idea; it must be brilliant and subdued at the same time, finely made, but with a secure sense of its own shape. A wisp was not what I wanted, not for Norah. Solidity, presence, was what I wanted, but in sinuous, ephemeral form. This was what Norah at seventeen, almost eighteen, was owed. She had always been a bravely undemanding child. Once, when she was four or five, she told me how she controlled her bad dreams at night. "I just turn my head around on the pillow," she said matter-of-factly, "and that changes the channel." She performed this act instead of calling out to us or crying; she solved her own nightmares and candidly exposed her original solution—which Tom and I took some comfort in but also, I confess, some amusement. I remember, with shame now, telling this story to friends, over coffee, over dinner, my brave little soldier daughter, shaping her soldierly life.

I seldom wear scarves myself, I can't be bothered, and

besides, whatever I put around my neck takes on the configuration of a Girl Scout kerchief, the knot working its
way straight to the throat, and the points sticking out
rather than draping gracefully downward. I was not clever
with accessories, I knew that about myself, and I was most
definitely not a shopper. I had never understood, in fact,
what it is that drives other women to feats of shopping perfection, but now I had a suspicion. It was the desire to
please someone fully, even one's self. It seemed to me that
my daughter Norah's future happiness now balanced not
on acceptance at Smith or the acquisition of a handsome
new boyfriend, but on the simple ownership of a particular article of apparel, which only I could supply. I had no
power over Smith or the boyfriend or, in fact, any real
part of her happiness, but I could provide something temporary and necessary: this dream of transformation, this
scrap of silk.

And there it was, relaxed over a fat silver hook in what
must have been the twentieth shop I entered. The little bell
rang; the updraught of potpourri rose to my nostrils, and
the sight of Norah's scarf flowed into view. It was patterned
from end to end with rectangles, each subtly out of alignment: blue, yellow, green, a kind of pleasing violet. And
each of these shapes was outlined by a band of black,
coloured in roughly as though with an artist's brush. I
found its shimmer dazzling and its touch icy and sensuous.
Sixty dollars. Was that all? I whipped out my VISA card

without a thought. My day had been well spent. I felt full of intoxicating power.

In the morning I took the train to Baltimore. I couldn't read on the train because of the jolting between one urban landscape and the next. Two men seated in front of me were talking loudly about Christianity, its sad decline, and they ran the words *Jesus Christ* together as though they were some person's first and second names—Mr. Christ, Jesus to the in-group.

In Baltimore, once again, there was little for me to do, but since I was going to see Gwen at lunch, I didn't mind. A young male radio host wearing a black T-shirt and gold chains around his neck asked me how I was going to spend the Offenden prize money. He also asked what my husband thought of the fact that I'd written a novel. (This is a question I've been asked before and for which I really must find an answer.) Then I visited the Book Plate (combination café and bookstore) and signed six books, and then, at not quite eleven in the morning, there was nothing more for me to do until it was time to meet Gwen.

Gwen and I had been in the same women's writing group back in Lancaster. In fact, she had been the informal but acknowledged leader for those of us who met weekly to share and "workshop" our writing. Poetry, memoirs, fiction; we brought photocopies of our work to these morning sessions, where over coffee and muffins—this was the age of muffins, the last days of the seventies—we kindly encouraged each other and offered tentative suggestions, such as "I think you're one draft from being finished" or "Doesn't character X enter the scene a little too late?" These critical crumbs were taken for what they were, the fumblings of amateurs. But when Gwen spoke we listened. Once she thrilled me by saying of something I'd written, "That's a fantastic image, that thing about the whalebone. I wish I'd thought of it myself." Her short fiction had actually been published in a number of literary quarterlies and there had even been one near-mythical sale, years earlier, to *Harper's*. When she moved to Baltimore five years ago to become writer-in-residence for a small women's college, our writers' group fell first into irregularity, and then slowly died away.

We'd kept in touch, though, the two of us. I wrote ecstatically when I happened to come across a piece of hers in *Three Spoons* which was advertised as being part of a novel-in-progress. She'd used my whalebone metaphor; I couldn't help noticing and, in fact, felt flattered. I knew about that novel of Gwen's—she'd been working on it for years—trying to bring a feminist structure to what was really a straightforward account of an early failed marriage. Gwen had made sacrifices for her young student husband, and he had betrayed her with his infidelities. In the early seventies, in the throes of love and anxious to satisfy his every demand, she had had her navel closed by a plastic surgeon because her husband complained that it smelled "off." The complaint, apparently, had been made only once, a sour, momentary whim, but out of some need to please or punish she became a woman without a navel, left with a flattish indentation in the middle of her belly, and this navel-less state, more than anything, became her symbol of regret and anger. She spoke of erasure, how her relationship to her mother—with whom she was on bad terms anyway—had been erased along with the primal mark of connection. She was looking into a navel recon-struction, she'd said in her last letter, but the cost was crim-inal. In the meantime, she'd retaken her unmarried name, Reidman, and had gone back to her full name, Gwendolyn.

She'd changed her style of dress too. I noticed that right away when I saw her seated at the Café Pierre. Her jeans and sweater had been traded in for what looked like large folds of unstitched, unstructured cloth, skirts and overskirts and capes and shawls; it was hard to tell precisely what they were. This cloth wrapping, in a salmon colour, extended to her head, completely covering her hair, and I wondered for an awful moment if she'd been ill, undergoing chemo-therapy and suffering hair loss. But no, there was a fresh, healthy, rich face. Instead of a purse she had only a lumpy plastic bag with a supermarket logo; that did worry me, especially because she put it on the table instead of setting it on the floor as I would have expected. It bounced slightly on the sticky wooden surface, and I remembered that she always carried an apple with her, a paperback or two, and her small bottle of cold-sore medication.

Of course I'd written to her when *My Thyme Is Up* was accepted for publication, and she'd sent back a postcard saying, "Well done, it sounds like a hoot."

I was a little surprised that she hadn't brought a copy for me to sign, and wondered at some point, halfway through my oyster soup, if she'd even read it. The college pays her shamefully, of course, and I know she doesn't have money for new books. Why hadn't I had Mr. Scribano send her a complimentary copy?

It wasn't until we'd finished our salads and ordered our coffee that I noticed she hadn't mentioned the book at all, nor had she congratulated me on the Offenden Prize. But perhaps she didn't know. The notice in the *New York Times* had been tiny. Anyone could have missed it.

It became suddenly important that I let her know about the prize. It was as strong as the need to urinate or swallow. How could I work it into the conversation?—maybe say something about Tom and how he was thinking of putting a new roof on our barn, and that the Offenden money would come in handy. Drop it in casually. Easily done.

"Right!" she said heartily, letting me know she already knew. "Beginning, middle, end." She grinned then.

She talked about her "stuff," by which she meant her writing. She made it sound like a sack of kapok. A magazine editor had commented on how much he liked her "stuff," and how her kind of "stuff" contained the rub of authenticity. There were always little linguistic surprises in her work, but more interesting to me were the bits of the world she brought to what she wrote, observations or incongruities or some sideways conjecture. She understood their value. "He likes the fact that my stuff is off-centre and steers a random course," she said of a fellow writer.

"No beginnings, middles, and ends," I supplied.

"Right," she said, "right." She regarded me fondly as though I were a prize pupil. Her eyes looked slightly pink at the corners, but it may have been a reflection from the cloth which cut a sharp line across her forehead.

I admire her writing. She claimed she had little imagination, that she wrote out of the material of her own life, but that she was forever on the lookout for what she called "putty." By this she meant the arbitrary, the odd, the ordinary, the mucilage of daily life that cements our genuine moments of being. I've seen her do wonderful riffs on buttonholes, for instance, the way they shred over time, especially on cheap clothes. And a brilliant piece on bevelled mirrors, and another on the smell of a certain set of wooden stairs from her childhood, wax and wood and reassuring cleanliness accumulating at the side of the story but not claiming any importance for itself.

She looked sad over her coffee, older than I'd remembered—but weren't we all?—and I could tell she was disappointed in me for some reason. It occurred to me I might offer her a piece of putty by telling her about the discovery I had made the day before, that shopping was not what I'd thought, that it could become a mission, even an art if one persevered. I had had a shopping item in mind; I had been presented with an unasked-for block of time; it might be possible not only to imagine this artefact, but to realize it.

"How many boutiques did you say you went into?" she asked, and I knew I had interested her at last.

"Twenty," I said. "Or thereabouts."

"Incredible."

"But it was worth it. It wasn't when I started out, but it became more and more worth it as the afternoon went on."

"Why?" she asked slowly. I could tell she was trying to twinkle a gram of gratitude at me, but she was closer to crying.

"To see if it existed, this thing I had in mind."

"And it did."

"Yes."

To prove my point I reached into my tote bag and pulled out the pale, puffy boutique bag. I unrolled the pink tissue paper on the table and showed her the scarf.

She lifted it against her face. Tears glinted in her eyes. "It's just that it's so beautiful," she said. And then she said, "Finding it, it's almost like you made it. You invented it, created it out of your imagination."

I almost cried myself. I hadn't expected anyone to understand how I felt.

I watched her roll the scarf back into the fragile paper. She took her time, tucking in the edges with her fingertips. Then she slipped the parcel into her plastic bag, tears spilling more freely now. "Thank you, darling Reta, thank you. You don't know what you've given me today."

But I did, I did.

But what does it amount to? A scarf, half an ounce of silk, maybe less, floating free in the world. I looked at Gwen/Gwendolyn, my old friend, and then down at my hands, my wedding band, my engagement ring, a little diamond thingamajig from the sixties. I thought of my three daughters and my mother-in-law and my own dead mother with her slack charms and the need she had to relax by painting china. Not one of us was going to get what we wanted. Imagine someone writing a play called *Death of a Saleswoman*. What a joke. We're so transparently in need of shoring up our little preciosities and our lisping pronouns, her, she. We ask ourselves questions, endlessly, but not nearly sternly enough. The world isn't ready for us yet; it hurts me to say that. We're too soft in our tissues, even you, Danielle Westerman, Holocaust survivor, cynic, and genius. Even you, Mrs. Winters, with your new, old useless knowledge. We are too kind, too willing, too unwilling too, reaching out blindly with a grasping hand but not knowing how to ask for what we don't even know we want.

Weather

———

M Y HUSBAND CAME HOME from work in a bad mood. There'd been a sudden downpour as he was driving in the direction of our village, and the rain, as usual, found its way into the distributor of his ancient car. Twice he'd had to stop at the side of the road, raise the hood, and apply a rag to the distributor cap.

His shirt was soaked by the time he came muttering up the back steps into the house, and his hair, what remains of it, was plastered to his head, exaggerating his already petulant look. To make matters worse, he'd heard on the car radio that the National Association of Meteorologists was going on strike the following day.

I cheered him up as best I could and fed him a hot meal even though it was the height of summer, his favourite braised lamb chops with mint sauce, the mint coming fresh from our own garden, that wild strip running along the side of the garage. "Never mind about the strike," I said, "it'll only last a day or two."

How wrong I was!

We kept tuned to the radio as the hours passed, but learned little more. Heated discussions were taking place, that was all we were told. For some reason these talks were kept highly secret. Conducted behind closed doors. Hush-hush.

"They're stuck on wages, I bet," my husband said. "This world of ours is getting greedier every year."

He likes to think he is above ordinary greed and materialistic longing, and he is. The neighbours are forever trading in their lawn mowers for bigger and better models, or investing in swimming pools, which he believes are pretentious and foolish, though I myself would be happy to think about installing a small concrete pool next to the porch, a glint of turquoise water meeting my eye as I glance out the window in the early morning; even a goldfish pond would give a kind of pleasure.

He cares nothing about such luxuries. He has his job at the plant nursery, his decent-though-troublesome car, his paid-for house, his vegetable garden, and he has a glassed-in porch from which he can watch the side-yard trees as they bend in the wind, a sight that never fails to rouse his spirits. I think—indeed he confided this to me in one of our rare tender moments—that he likes to imagine the immensity of the trees' root systems, plunging downward beneath the surface of the complacent lawn, then branching sideways, and adding foot by fibrous foot to a complex network of tentacles that grab at the earth's clumped particles, securely anchoring the great oaks and maples, never mind how rambunctious the wind gets, never mind the weather warnings. Roots, he said to me the evening we had this strange conversation, perform the job they're designed to do, no more, no less. They don't take time off for coffee and a smoke, and they don't bellyache about remuneration. (You need to understand that my husband is the sort of man who appreciates a high degree of application and tenacity. He wishes that his fellow human beings were just as dutiful and as focused in their day-to-day lives as he himself is.)

The first twenty-four hours of the strike stretched to forty-eight and then seventy-two. My own opinion was that the meteorologists were holding out for a better pension plan. Retirement and pensions are all everyone talks about these days, though I'm frightened of retirement myself, my husband's retirement that is. What will he do with himself, a man with his ever-present tide of irascibility? "It's probably working conditions they're quibbling about," my husband barked. His own work conditions suit him perfectly, since he is an outdoors man by nature. I sometimes sense, but then I have known him for a long time, that he can barely distinguish between where his body stops and the elements begin—though he does, as I say, hate getting soaked in the rain.

The first week of the strike affected us both. There was talk about arbitration but, as is often the case, it came to nothing. Meanwhile without weather, we struggled against frustration and boredom. I had never before thought about deprivation on this scale, but I soon discovered that one day is exactly like the next, hour after hour of featureless, tensionless air. We were suddenly without seasonal zest, without hourly variation, without surprise and complaint, dislocated in time and space. There was nothing to press upon the skin, nothing for the body to exert itself against, nothing that satisfied. The idea of umbrellas was suddenly laughable (though we didn't laugh, at least I don't remember laughing). And there was no thought of drawing the living-room blinds against the sun.

The garden more or less disowned its responsibilities. The row of tomato plants—Mexican Ecstasy was what we were trying out this year—bore well enough, though the tomatoes themselves refused to ripen. Ripeness requires long periods of bright, warm light, as everyone knows, but for the duration of the strike we were stuck in a bland width of greyness with day after day of neither heat nor cold. "At least we don't have to worry about frost," my husband grumbled in one of his reasonable moments, but his forehead was warped with anger, and his patience further tried by yet another extension of the strike.

Deadlocked, they said on the eleven o'clock news; the two sides still miles apart.

A neighbour—he owns one of those satellite dishes and is therefore able to tune in to five hundred news sources—told us the government was thinking of calling in the troops. What good would that do? I thought. "What good would that do?" my husband said loudly. He'd gone off his food by now. Nothing I put on the table seemed right, not my special potato salad, not even my New Orleans gumbo. Winter fare, summer fare, it didn't matter. The cherry vanilla ice cream we like so much withheld its flavour during this weatherless period, as did my spiced beef stew and dumplings. Our own green beans from the garden, needless to say, shrivelled before we could pick them.

Like children, we were uncertain as to how to clothe ourselves in the morning. Longs or shorts? Wool or cotton? Denim or polyester? My green short-sleeved rayon dress that I'm quite fond of—and so too is my husband, if I can read his eyes—seemed inappropriate, out of place, too loaded with interseasonal deliberation. As for his own work shirts, should he put on the plaid flannel or the boxy open-weave? How were we to decide, and what did it matter anyway? This lack of mattering smarted like a deerfly's sting. I found it impossible to look directly at my husband during those early morning decisions.

Something that surprised me was how much I missed the heft of daily barometric reassurance, and this was

particularly curious since all my life the humidity index has
felt obscurely threatening, informing us in a firm, masculine radio voice that we were either too wet or too dry for
our own good. For our health and happiness. For the con-
tinuation of the planet. No one ever indicated we might
reach a perfect state of humidity/dryness balance, and perhaps there is no such thing. But to be *unsituated* in terms of
moisture, without either dampness or aridity to serve as a
guide, is to be nowhere. The skin of my inner thighs was
suddenly in a state of ignorance, not knowing how to react.
My breasts itched, but the itch could not be relieved by
scratching or by the application of calamine lotion. I mentioned to my husband a rustic barometer I remembered
from childhood, a mechanism consisting of a tiny wooden
house with two doors. When the humidity was high and
rain imminent, the right-hand door opened and a little
lean boy-doll, mild-faced and costumed in Alpine dress,
appeared. When it was dry, a smiling little girl swung into
view, promising sunshine.

My husband, his elbows on the kitchen table, listened.
His nicely trimmed beard twitched and vibrated, and I
thought for a minute he was about to ask a question, raising a point that, in fact, had just occurred to me: Why
should the little boy signify rain and the girl sunshine?
Did humidity and dryness possess such specific and bio-
logically assigned qualities, each of which could be measured and interpreted?

But all he said was, "You never told me that before."

"You never asked me," I said, exasperated.

The strike was into its third week, and I found myself impatient with the dulling and rounding of each twenty-four-hour segment, marked by a pencil check on the calendar and nothing else. Our lives have always been uncertain owing to my husband's disposition, and mine too perhaps, but at least we'd had the alternating rhythm of light and darkness to provide continuity.

To live frictionlessly in the world is to understand the real grief of empty space. Nostalgically I recalled the fluting of air currents in the late afternoon hours, hissing against the backyard shrubs and the fetid place where we stashed the garbage cans. And the interlace of heat and coolness on my cheeks as I carried home my sacks of groceries. I wondered if my husband remembered how, only days ago, the wind used to slide against the west side of the porch, arriving in chunks or else splinters, and how it rattled the glass in the window frames, serving up for us a nervous, silvery sort of evening music that produced, simultaneously, a sense of worry and of consolation.

I felt an urge to voice such thoughts aloud, but, as usual, was uncertain in my husband's presence. To speak of propulsive sunshine and solemn shade, and the jolts of expectation that hang between the two, would be to violate a code of intimacy we had long since established.

What I remember most from that painful, weatherless

period is the sky's mute bulk of stillness. Day after day it continued in its building up—pressureless, provisional, and, most heartbreaking of all, exhibiting a cloudlessness that was unrelieved. Clouds. After a month I began to think that perhaps clouds were something I had only imagined. How could anything exist as lovely and as whimsical as these masses of whipped cream that transformed themselves an hour later into bright rapturous streamers of scratched air?

I dreamed one night of a tower of cloud rising in the vivid setting sun, its fringed edges painted the deep-fried gold of apple fritters, and, at the centre, shading inward with a sly, modulated subtlety, the dense pewtery purple that announces a storm either approaching or receding, it didn't matter which. By morning I was sobbing into my pillow, but my husband, who had risen earlier, was not there to offer comfort.

We woke and slept. My husband's job was cancelled for the duration of the strike, and so we were thrown more and more together. We tended to bump into each other around the house, getting on each other's nerves, and one day I discovered him on the porch staring out at the vacant air; he was stooped and looked older than he is, and on impulse I laced my hands around the bulk of his back, pressing the side of my face against his shirt.

Later that same day we heard the news about the settlement of the strike. It seemed the meteorologists had wanted

nothing all along but the public's appreciation and gratitude, and this now had been unanimously promised and
even written into their contract.

My husband and I slept in each other's arms that night,
and it was shortly after midnight when we were stirred out
of profound unconsciousness by a breeze loosened in the
elms and carried to us through the mesh of the house's various window screens.

Then, after an hour or so, drifting in and out of wake-
fulness, we heard, or perhaps imagined, the ballet-slipper
sound of raindrops on the garage roof. A bank of coolness
and damp arrived together at first dawn, and entered the
valved darkness of our lungs, mine and his.

I touched his mouth with my thumb then, rubbing it
back and forth. We held on to each other tightly during
those minutes, feeling the essence of weather blow through
us, thinking the same thoughts, and I remembered that
thing which, for stretches of dull time, I tend to forget. That
despite everything, the two of us have learned the trick of
inhabiting parallel weather systems, of making for ourselves—and no one else—snowstorms in August, of bringing into view the air of autumn, whenever we wish, the icy
pain at the bottom of every breath, and then arriving at the
gateway of illogical, heat-enhanced January, and imagining
the April wind on my face, and his too, which is no louder
nor more damaging than a dozen friendly bees, so that we
have curiosity enough to rise and begin another day.

Flatties

Their Various Forms and Uses

———

A TRADITIONAL FLATTY IS composed of flour, fat, still-water, and salt. The flour commonly used in our islands derives from *bjøerne*, a hearty local barley, almost black in colour and longer in the grain than Elsewhere barley. *Bjøerne* is gathered by the young boys of the isles in middle or late summer, depending on wind and weather conditions, and winnowed on the first three days following St. Ulaf's Night, except during those years in which the full moon precedes the usual holy oblations. On these rare occasions winnowing may occur at any hour or day, provided a hollyberry candle is first lit in the barnplace opening. Ordinary tallow will suffice should hollyberry prove scarce.

In the old days flour for flatties was ground in a stone quern. Today the intercession of wind or water is more frequently invoked, and it is said that the Island of Strell mills a goodly portion of its flour nowadays with the assistance of wavelight.

You will already be acquainted with the longitude and latitude of our archipelago, as well as its annual rainfall, and so I will confine myself here to a few domestic particulars. The islands of our homeplace are Naust, Spoy, Strell, Upper Strell, Cailee, Papa Cailee, Nack, Breen, Little Breen (where the barelegs live), and Lum, my own place of birth and lifebeing. Flatties are consumed by the peoples of all these islands except for Naust, where inhabitants decline to eat them. They fear even to touch them. Instead, a small loaf-bread constitutes their chief nourishment, a mixture of crumbled meal and milk over which a prayer is uttered so that its volume doubles and trebles. The people of Naust fasten horseshoes to the hooves of their draught animals in order to protect the beastfeet from poisons that are stirred up by the action of plough and harrow.

The indigenous folk of Strell and Upper Strell are alike in their fondness for flatties that are shaped in a circle with a small depression in the middle. Their horseshoes too reflect an inclination for circularity, the two traditional points having long since merged so that there is no visible break or separation. Boys are presented with their horseshoes at the age of twelve, girls at fourteen.

The small Island of Spoy has not yet adopted the Lum-Bode. The people there rely instead on baking their flatties in a vertical passageway of shaped stone or brick which is said to carry smoke away from their dwellings. They nail their horseshoes over these passageways before a baking takes place, being careful that the prongs point skyward in a gesture of respect and also imprecation. Flatties are sometimes referred to by the oldenfolk of Spoy as *fletcake* or *platter-brød*, but these locutions are now in decline.

Though flatties abound on the Island of Cailee, it is believed there are no women among the inhabitants from whom sailors may purchase a foodhoard. These brave sea-men must set sail without a supply of flatties and without the womanly benedictions that protect other island folk from disorder and caprice. Caileeans wear their horseshoes suspended from a thong of leather around their necks, and before a voyage they bend forward in a deep bow, kissing the curve of iron in the ceremonial way, and in this manner preserve all that blesses and encourages them in their lives.

On the Isle of Papa Cailee, flatties are baked commu-nally, owing to the small number of inhabitants. By tradi-tion, Caileean men stir the flour and water together in a great pot, after which the women gather together and add the needed fat and salt. A single horseshoe is placed at the bottom of the baking pan for the purpose of enhancing flavour and goodness. Before being eaten, the flatties of Papa Cailee are spread with beehoney and folded in quarters.

The dwellers of Nack are partial to the savour of strong salt. Their flatties, therefore, possess a unique character, and a heat that is teasing to the tongue. Preserved fish is sometimes pressed between a pair of Nack-flatties and this *skørpe*, as it is called, is eaten from the hand in the open air. Nackfolk, when they are at leisure, enjoy a pursuit in which they hurl their horseshoes in the direction of a stationary wooden peg. Men, women, and children also are known to participate in this activity.

On the westward-lying Isle of Breen, flatties are baked but once a year. The baking takes place in the old chapel-yard, and the first flatty to emerge from the bakeoven is broken over the ground where the thighbone of Saint Gårtrude is buried. There is no stone to mark this place; instead, a circle of horseshoes serves to remind folk that they are treading near holy-earth and cautions them to observe silence and to abide in a state of peace with their neighbours.

Just half-a-daysail north lies Little Breen, where flatties are cooked on a griddle instead of an oven. They are eaten three times a day, and also at the feasts of sowing and harvesting. Those folk who fall sick are given flatties that are first soaked in sourmilk and sprinkled with the fine-ground meat of acorns. When a death occurs, the people of Little Breen throw a horseshoe into the sea so that the soul of the departed will be anchored to the earth and not lose its way.

Here on the Isle of Lum we prefer to add one or two eggs to each baking of flatties, most especially in the summertime when hens are clean-laying. A well-polished horseshoe is placed beneath the straw of each nest, and this greatly encourages the eggyield. It is the very young children who collect these eggs and carry them in baskets to the bakehouse. They never stumble, no egg is ever broken. Children born on islands differ from Elsewhere children in that they are knowing of each rock and fencepost of their homeplace, of every field-corner and doorway, every spit of sand and beach pebble. This knowledge imbues them with good health and strong trust, so that they are able to look out across the widewater and observe the wonder and diversity of our earthhome. May it ever be so.

Dying for Love

———

M Y FIRST THOUGHT this morning is for Beth, how on Earth she'll cope now that Ted's left her for the dancer Charlotte Brown. I ask myself, what resources does a woman like Beth have, emotional resources? Will she get through the first few days and nights? The nights will be terrible for her, I'm sure of that, long and heavy.

For four years they've been together, almost five, perhaps longer. Habits accrue in that time, especially habits of the night when bodies and their routines get driven into hard rituals of washed skin, brushed teeth, programmes of solemnity, then the light switch flicked off, then, *then* the orchestrated folding back of the almost weightless cotton blanket—for it's spring now, late May—and the mattress buttons pushing upward. Five years gives time to study and absorb and take on the precise rhythms of another person's

breathing pattern and to accommodate their night postures, whether they sprawl or thrash or curl up tight. Beth
curls, but sinuously; her backbone makes a long smiling
capital C on the bedsheet, or used to, before Ted told her
he was leaving her for Charlotte.

Before bed, ever since Ted left, she drinks a cup of hot
milk. This milk holds a dose of self-destruction, since she
hates the taste and can only choke it down if it's accompanied by a slice of toast spread with peanut butter, and this
exacerbates her weight problem, which was one of the issues
between her and Ted. He has an unreasoning fear of fat,
though from a certain angle his own face looks fleshy and
indulged. Charlotte Brown the dancer is so thin it breaks
your heart. Even off her points, walking diagonally across a
room, she has a tripping look of someone balancing on little glass stilts; also a pair of hip bones shaved down like
knives, also a high thin ribbony voice.

Beth's met Charlotte twice, once at a pre-performance
party, which is also where Ted first met her, and again,
recently, when the three of them, Ted, Beth, and Charlotte,
had a drink together in a bar called the Captain's Bridge and
discussed the surprisingly long list of domestic details that
now needed reordering. Ted and Charlotte are planning to
be married, something Ted and Beth in their five years had
never considered, at least Ted had not. On this particular
evening, out of embarrassment possibly, he lifted his glass
and attempted a witticism so derivative—"You only get

married for the first time once"—that Beth pressed her hands to the sides of her head, causing her blouse to rip under one arm.

Ted took out a pencil and note pad. There was the lease to consider; he would pay his share through the end of June. And some stemware to split up, and two sets of oven mitts. "We won't discuss oven mitts." Beth said this nicely, with dignity. Then a desk chair, his. A brass umbrella stand, hers. A monkey fern that Ted claimed to have nursed through a bad spell after Beth neglected it. There was also, at the bottom of the list, a certain six-cup, hard-to-replace aluminum coffeepot.

Beth had planned to be relaxed and offhand for this meeting; that was the reason she was wearing an old red cotton blouse with buttons fastening on the side. She worked hard to keep the toads from leaping out of her mouth. She kept her hand away from the dish of smoked pecans and held her head bravely erect as though she were sniffing a long-stemmed rose, a trick she learned from an article in a beauty magazine. Airily preoccupied, she managed to convey the impression that she was about to rush off to meet friends in a restaurant, close friends, old friends, and that she was already late and would probably have to take a cab, but that she was perfectly prepared to bear this expense, happy in fact to part with her last ten dollars, so eager was she for sympathetic companionship, to be among her own kind of people. She glanced frequently at her watch, at the same time quietly maintaining her right to the six-cup coffeepot.

"I don't drink coffee," Charlotte Brown said in a dazed, injured voice.

"All right then, keep the coffeepot," Ted said, none too gently, causing Beth to grab her jacket, white linen, and rush out the door without saying good-bye or wishing the two of them happiness and good fortune in the years ahead.

Later she thought of stuffing one of Ted's stray socks in the coffeepot and mailing it to his new address. Or filling it with her birth-control pills and leaving it at his door. Or donating it to a money raiser for the victims of AIDS.

Instead she put the coffeepot on the top shelf of a cupboard where she would hardly ever have to look at it.

I find it difficult to imagine how Beth will cope emotionally. Nevertheless, despite her insomnia, she somehow manages to get up most mornings, get herself dressed, and go to work in the office of a very large swimwear factory. A woman named Jennifer Downs who works in the same office pressed a little packet into Beth's hand one day. Sleeping pills, she whispered. Just a few. To get you through the next couple of weeks. You need your sleep, you need to keep yourself from falling apart.

Beth has a bottle of gin in her cupboard and wonders what would happen if she took all twelve pills plus the gin. She doesn't know. I don't either. Probably nothing would happen; this is what she decides anyway—nothing. But just in case she empties the gin bottle down the kitchen sink. The pills she grinds in the disposal unit.

Then she wanders into her bathroom, her hot milk in hand, and permits herself an admiring look in the ripply mirror, but nonchalantly, coolly, out of the corner of her eye. What she sees is the profile of someone who had considered joining that tiny company of women who have died for love. She salutes the side of her face with her thick pottery mug, across which is written the word SMILE.

Life is a thing to be cherished, she thinks, and this thought, slender as a handrail, gets her through one more night.

But then there's Lizzie in Somerset; my fears for Lizzie grow day by day. Her predicament is clear and so is her fate, although I can perhaps imagine a way to assist her in the avoidance of that fate.

It is now a fortnight since Ned quit the lodgings where the two of them have sheltered these last several months. Ever since his departure Lizzie has grieved, and repeated over and over to herself their final hour together, a long damp scene in which Ned's confession of temptation and weakness had gone on and on, running out of his mouth so wastefully, and all for her account, when a single phrase would have done: he was sodden with love, and for a music hall performer named Carlotta. When he pronounced the word *love*, the little muscles around his lips strained towards a decency that surprised her.

The first shock of silence once Lizzie found herself truly alone in the room was chilling. She dealt, finally, with her necessary calculations, adding and subtracting while pacing the length of the pink wallpapered room overlooking the filthy cobbled street.

Small rented rooms such as this have the power to accumulate sharp clarities, particularly the relentless press of time passing, how it can never be turned backwards. Lizzie's small breasts, over which Neddie had sighed with disappointment, or so she fancied, were now engorged, swollen against her muslin bodice, their tips shivering with hurt. She was only eighteen, but of country stock, and knew the signs. An older sister, married and living in Oxfordshire, had spoken to her gently of female vulnerability, of the moon and its controlling power, but this was before Neddie made his appearance in the region.

He was a manufacturer's representative from Bolton. His hours were irregular. It seemed he could work when he liked, and more often he went his rounds in the early evening when, as he said, people were most easily persuaded in their buying and selling. His shirts—he possessed three—had seen better days, but his coat, which was of dark woollen stuff, and elegant, and was buttoned in the new single-breasted way, spoke of reliability. So too did his gold

watch and chain and the glossy manner in which he fingered these objects. Lizzie worried about his shoes, their
scraped toes and cracked uppers, wondering what, if anything, they signified.

He teased her with foolish compliments and practised
on her a perverse magic, for, by praising her simplicity, he
urged her to abandon it. By exclaiming over her devotion,
he hinted that her pretty ways fell somehow short of full
womanly expression. Her sincerity of affection was so forth-
right, so cheerful, candid, and unstinting, that he fell into a
sulk and accused her of loving everyone else as well as she
loved him. His restlessness, his tapping foot, his drumming
fingers, the tiny working muscles around his mouth
beseeched her to give up that token he most truly desired,
and finally, in the cushiony orchard, under a sky of depth-
less black, she surrendered.

Now she sat in a small room counting off days. A series
of pictures tripped through her head, joining the pink
flowers on the wall and receding finally into a continuous
blur of grief. She has told Mrs. Hanna who keeps the lodg-
ing house that her husband will pay the rent as soon as he
returns from a brief journey to Derbyshire, a journey neces-
sitated by a sudden illness in her mother's family. Poor creature, said Mrs. Hanna with her munching gums, poor
creature, and Lizzie has turned these words over in her
mind at least a hundred times.

Late one spring night, in the tender darkness, she flung

a cloak across her shoulders, swiftly pinned a hat to her head, and strode towards the site of the New Bridge.

The New Bridge is a wonder. Great iron spans swing between tapering stone piles in a manner so harmonious that mountains are brought to mind, and feudal strongholds and brave deeds. The graceful railings are decorated with iron Tritons and plunging sea creatures, thrusting their green painted heads boldly forward and interlacing their scaly tails. Far below the flooded river roars and sings.

A yellowish light now forms on the bridge railing, a spumy brightness as clear as paint, but cut over and across by shapes of heavy leaves and whip-like branches, and above them a watery aisle outlined and tinted by a three-quarters-full moon. *Now*, Lizzie whispers. And hoists herself up among the moulded mermaids. Now!

But two thoughts quickly intervene. First, that she is a remarkably able swimmer. Her father, who drank, who told lies, who pocketed money he had no right to, who blasphemed, who could scarcely read, who was prideful and superstitious—this same man had taught each of his seven children, daughters as well as sons, to swim. He stood waist high in pond water and supported their bodies with the shelf of his broad arms, encouraging them to kick for their lives and thrash and keep their heads above the treacherous surface; over and over until they had it right, until it became second nature—which is why Lizzie knows that the moment she breaks through the white foam, a phantom courage will drive her smoothly and swiftly in the direction of the river bank.

Her second thought is for her hat, which is yellow straw with a band of cut-felt violets around its crown, given her by the Oxford sister on her last birthday. She holds the hat in little regard, but senses at the same time the absurdity, the impossibility, of drowning in such a hat. Nor will she leave it on the bridge railing to be picked up by the first passerby.

Suddenly, like a wave riding well above its fellows, her sorrow collapses. She smiles, licks her lips, and turns her back on the tide of river water with its glints and crescents and riding knots of gold. Down there in the swirling currents her dear Neddie's behaviour is suspended. Not only that, but she imagines possibilities of rescue. Mrs. Hanna. Her Oxford sister. Some few remaining coins in the bottom of a purse. Who can tell.

It is to my advantage that I can discard the possibilities Lizzie can't even imagine. All she understands is that both love and the lack of love can be supported. Loneliness might even be useful, she thinks—and clinging to this slender handrail of hope she readjusts her hat and strikes off down the road.

Elsewhere, much nearer home, a woman named Elizabeth is lying on her bed in the middle of the afternoon with a plastic dry cleaner's bag drawn up over her face, like a blanket in freezing weather. She is no longer young. A week ago she apprehended herself, not directly in a mirror, but by catching hold of her image, almost by chance, in the presence of its encircling flesh, and realized that this disintegrating quilted envelope would accompany her to the end, and that she had lost forever the power to stir ardour.

Nevertheless she is surprisingly calm, breathing almost indifferently against the thin plastic covering. She inhales and exhales experimentally, playfully, observing the way the membrane puckers and clings, then withdraws at her pleasure. She has been married for twenty-five years, and is still married, to a man who no longer loves her; it's gone, it's used up, it's worn away, and there's nothing to bring it back; half her despair derives from knowing that this thing that's collapsed so suddenly in her has been dead to him for years, and she thinks how much more bearable an abrupt abandonment of love would have been.

How much more acceptable, like a cleanly applied knife, if he were to leave her for someone else, one of the secretaries in his office, for instance, some girl with a swaying, gliding pelvis, with carelessly bundled dark massy hair and bright coral mouth and fingernails—perhaps her name would be Coral as well, Coral of the swervy body and rhythmic hands who would bring about an honest spasm of betrayal and not this slow airless unassuageable absence.

She tries hard to picture the two of them together, her husband and this woman Coral, and for an instant a colour photo flickers on her eyelids. But she has trouble keeping it in focus. Instead she is imagining the legions of other women who have almost died for love, how they are all fetched from the same province of illusion, the same fraying story, and how they employ the same shadeless metaphors. A tragic narrative, unbearable, except that the recurrent episodes—of ecstasy, shock, loss, and lament—are similarly, cunningly, hinged to a saving capacity for digression and recovery, for the ability to be called back by clamorous objects and appointments. A woman at the end of love, after all, is not the same as a woman at the end of her tether. She has the power to create parallel stories that offer her a measure of comfort.

Already the plastic bag has loosened its hold and slipped down below her face, a bag that only yesterday enclosed a heavy grey overcoat, her husband's, and was carried home by Elizabeth herself from the dry cleaner's in a nearby shopping mall and put away in a cedar closet until next winter.

Close to the dry cleaner's establishment—her brain drifts and skitters as it refills with oxygen—is a florist's where she sometimes buys cut flowers, and next to the florist's is a delicatessen where rare honeys and olives can be found. She is a woman whose life is crowded with not-unpleasant errands and with the entrapment of fragrant, familiar, and sometimes enchanting items, all of which possess a reassuring, measurable weight and volume.

Not that this is much of a handrail to hang on to—she knows that, and so do I—but it is at least continuous, solid, reliable as a narrative in its turnings and better than no handrail at all.

Ilk

—

B Y NOW EVERYONE'S seen the spring issue of *Ficto-Factions*, page 146, in which G.T.A., whoever he/she may be, summarises the various papers that were presented at the recent NWUS Conference on Narrativity and Notation. Put your finger on the third paragraph of the summary, move it halfway down, and you'll see that the astute and androgynous G.T.A. refers to me by name. The bit about "the new theory of narrative put forward at NWUS and how it illustrates the atemporal paradigms of L. Porter and his ilk."

It happens that I am L. Porter—but you already know that. It's printed right here on my name tag.

I prefer to be direct in my responses, so I'll admit straightaway that an inexplicable gust of sadness passed

through me when I came across G.T.A's pointed but
oblique mention, and I realized too after some reflection
that I was subtly injured to see myself accompanied by a
faithful, though imaginary, pool of "ilk." By the way, that
should be *her* ilk, not *his*, the *L* in my name standing for
Lucy, after my no longer living and breathing Aunt Lucy.
(Traditionally, of course, Lucy has been a female name, and
one that comes embedded with complementary echoes of
lacy, and also the lazy-daisy womb of its final *y*.) Nevertheless, my good friends, as distinct from my "ilk," have
persuaded me that if I'm really serious about getting tenure
I'd better sign my published articles with my initial only. In
these days of affirmative action, Lucy Porter gets interviews,
plenty of them, but L. Porter gets people to read her "ilk-
ish" ideas about narrative.

So where exactly do I stand, then, on narrative enclo-
sures? Or, to put it another way, how small can ficto-
fragments get without actually disappearing? First, forget
all that spongy Wentworthian whuss about narrative as
movement. A narrative isn't something you pull along like
a toy train, a perpetually thrusting indicative. It's this little
subjunctive cottage by the side of the road. All you have to
do is open the door and walk in. Sometimes you might
arrive and find the door ajar. That's always nice. Other
times you crawl in through a window. You look around,
pick yourself a chair, sit down, relax. You're there. Chrysalis
collapses into cognition. You apprehend the controlling

weights and counterweights of separate acts and objects. No
need to ask for another thing.

All right, most of us know this instinctively. Where
Dick Wentworth (R. S. Wentworth, teacher/scholar/critic)
goes wrong is in confusing narrative containment with
sequentiality and its engagé/dégagé assumptions concern-
ing directedness, the old shell game, only with new flags
attached. "Look," I explain to him at the ANRAA Sym-
posium in January—we collide while checking our coats at
the opening night wine-and-cheese reception—"a fictive
module doesn't need a fully rigged sailing vessel. A footstool
is all it needs. Or a longing for a footstool."

And I'm not just talking minimalism here. I'm saying
that fiction's clothes can be folded so small they'd fit inside a glass marble. You could arrange them on those little
plastic doll hangers and hook them over the edge of Dick
Wentworth's name tag. There's a bud of narrativity opening
up right there behind the linked lettering, as there is
beneath all uniquely arbitrary signs. There's (A) the dick-
ness of Dick, all it says and gestures toward. And (B) the
sir/surname, Wentworth, with its past-tense failure rubbing
up against the trope of privilege, not to mention (C) the
underground wire pulling on Jane Austen's *Persuasion*. Like
it or not, Professor Wentworth's name bursts with narrative
chlorophyll. His beard, his belly, they're separate stories.
His pale face too. A wide bashful puzzled face. His wife
killed herself. Someone told me that at last year's meeting.

I watch him draw his scarf slowly into the tunnel of his coat sleeve before handing it over to the coat-check person, all the way in, with the little fringed ends hanging out at the shoulder and cuff. His scarf is a cheap tan scarf and doesn't deserve this kind of care. He turns to me. His mouth opens. "As Barthes says—"

"Excuse me," I say. "I'm starving. That looks like shrimp over there."

"So, how's the job search going?"

"And real champagne," I say gushingly. Ilkishly.

My Aunt Lucy, already referred to, had a short life, thirty-six years, then cancer got her, grabbed her. She lived in Bedford, New Hampshire, where she worked as a secretary-receptionist in a piano factory. She couldn't play the piano herself, not a note. She wasn't very bright. She wasn't eccentric, either. She almost never remembered to send me birthday cards or small gifts. The alignment of her teeth was only so-so. So why do I insist that her skinny maladroit cancer-eaten body housed an epic, a drama, a romance, a macro-fiction, a ficto-universe? Because narrativity is ovarian, not ejaculatory as so many of our contemporary teachers/scholars/critics tend to assume.

I give you my poor old relation as an example only, putting my trust in the simplifying afterlight of metaphor which is all we have. The point is, as I try to explain to Professor Wentworth: "Narrative fullness thrives in the interstices of nano-seconds. Or nano-people, like my aunt.

Though oddly enough, Professor Wentworth, I was crazy about her."

"It's Dick. Please. Don't you remember our last conversation when we agreed—?"

"Dick, yes."

"Ovarian? You were saying—?"

"I should have said egg. Egg's a good word. A single cell—"

"A single cell—hmmm." He strokes his chin at this point, stroke, stroke.

"—holds the surfaces of the real."

"But. But, Lucy, tension absolutely cannot be created in a vacuum."

Is this a trick? Starting a sentence with a double "but"? I call that aggressive. Or else aggression's reverse side, which is helplessness. "Look, Professor Wentworth, Dick. There's plenty of high-octane tension flowing between the simple states of being and non-being—"

"Which points," he says, "to the other side of this discourse."

"Every discourse is born of a micro-discourse," say I, wanting to press his sad effusions into something ardent and orderly. Something useful.

"Uh-huh."

There is only one shrimp left on the plate. It lies curled on its side, paler than a shrimp should be, and misshapen. I feel a yearning to know its story.

Also, I can't help noticing that its ridged shrimpy curl matches almost exactly the configurative paisley splotches on Professor Wentworth's tie. I stare at that tie, something makes me. The mixed blues and reds strike me as boyishly courageous, but it is the knot that brings a puddle of tears to my throat. Or rather, it is the way he, Dick Wentworth, keeps touching that knot as he speaks, applying pressure with his thumb, pushing against the spread stiffness of buttoned oxford cloth and into the erect column of the neck itself. A good enough neck, soapy, a forty-year-old neck, or thereabouts. I remember that his wife hanged herself. From a water pipe. In the basement of their house. In Ithaca, New York.

"I'm afraid I don't quite see—" he begins, his thumb rising once again, preparing to push.

His whole life seems gathered in that little silky harbour. Mine too, for some reason. Probably the champagne fizzing up into my nose.

Did I make up that part about the water pipe? Me and my ilk and I, we're given to such exiguous notation. Doublings. Triangulations. Narrativistically speaking, our brush-strokes outreach our grasp.

"You've probably heard," says Dick Wentworth, "that we, ahem, have an opening in the department for next year. It's, hmmmm, in composition and rhetoric, but reassignment is always an option," he continues, "once tenure is confirmed," he goes on, "and you might, if you will excuse me for saying so," he concludes, "be ready for—"

I did say, didn't I, that my Aunt Lucy was thirty-six when she withered away? Exactly the age I will be in four years and three ilkly months.

Cross that last bit out. There's no room for self-pity in the satellite-bounced fictions of today. Ellipsis, though crownless, is queen. I remind Dick Wentworth of this insight.

"I'm afraid I didn't quite catch what you said. This noise, all these people, that execrable music."

"I said I'd give it some thought."

"What?"

"The position. The post. The post/position."

"Oh."

He was away attending another conference when it happened. The combined SWUS/NWUS biannual, the year he gave his paper on "Stasis and Static in Early Twentieth Century Cowboy Imbroglios." Brilliant. Shedding light on. Now it seems he can't forgive himself for signing up for the post-conference mini-session on the couplet.

"Really? The couplet?"

"The line, actually."

She'd been dead, apparently, for just twenty-four hours when he got home. The police, even in off-the-map places like Ithaca, are good at figuring out things like the amount of water left in the body cells after the heart stops. It decreases at a known rate. Experts have considered this, done graphs and so on.

"The line, you said?"

"Well, perhaps I should have said the word."

Of course she left a note. On the kitchen table probably. Or pinned to her bathrobe. It doesn't matter where. What matters is what the note said. Only one word, rumour has it. Scratched in pen or pencil or chalk, scratched into the laminated tabletop, into the wood panelling of the basement rec room, with a nail, with a nail file, with a piece of glass, scratched on her wrists—it doesn't matter.

"Salary?"

"Small."

"How small? Do you mean, hmmmm, ridiculously small?"

"Annual increments, though. And benefits."

"Benefits!"

What matters, at least to L. Porter and her ilk, is the exact word she left behind. Its orthography, its referents. The word is the central modality, after all. The narrational heart.

There are infinite possibilities. A dictionary of possibilities. You'd think that little scratched word would come scuttling towards me on jointed legs, wouldn't you, eager to make itself registered. It might have been something accusing (betrayal). Or confessional (regret). Or descriptive (depression), or existential (lost, loose, lust)? or dialogic (a simple good-bye). No, all too predictable. Reactive rather than initiative.

My guess is that she left some kind of disassociative verbal unit: leaf, water, root, fire, fish.

"Love."

"What did you says?" To narrativize is to step back from spontaneous expression, even as one consolidates the available, accessible, amenable material of the world.

"Love," he says again, looking down, sideways, then up at the ceiling fan, ready to withdraw his narratival disjuncture and press forward to other, wider topics.

"Pardon?"

"We'd love to have you aboard."

The spine of the final shrimp is parked between his front teeth now. Sitting there rather sweetly, in fact, though it makes it difficult to catch his next words. "My ilk is your ilk" is what I think I heard.

Stop!

THE QUEEN HAS dropped out of sight. At the busiest time of the court season too, what with the Admiral's Ball coming up, and the People's Picnic. No one knows where she's disappeared to. Has she gone to the seaside? Unthinkable. A person who is sensitive to salt water, to sand, to beach grass and striped canvas, does not traipse off to the seaside. Well, where, then? It used to be that she would spend a few days in the mountains in late summer. She loved the coolness, she said, the grandeur. But now her sinuses react to balsam and pine. And to the inclines of greenness and shadow.

No, she is a stay-at-home queen. A dull queen. Not exactly beloved, but a queen who is nevertheless missed when she is absent. People are starting to talk, to wonder. They understand that the pollen count is high, and so it is not unreasonable that she remain enclosed in her tower. But why have the windows been bricked in? Can it be that she has developed an intolerance to sunlight too? Poor soul, and just at the turning of the year with the air so fine and pale.

Music, of course, has been anathema for years. Bugles, trumpets, and drums were confiscated in the first triannulus of her reign, and stringed instruments—violins, cellos— inevitably followed. It was heartbreaking to see, especially the moment when the Queen's own harp was smashed by hammers and the pieces buried deep in the palace garden.

Simple nourishment has always been for her a form of torture. Fruits and vegetables, meat and milk bring on duodenal spasms, but, worse, she is unable to bear the shape of a spoon in her mouth. The finest clothing rubs and chafes. The perfume of flowers causes her to faint, and even oxygen catches in her windpipe so that she coughs and chokes and calls for the court physician.

Ah, the physician! What grave responsibility that man bears. It was he, after all, who first recognized the danger of ragweed and banished it from the realm. Then roses. Then common grass and creeping vines. It was he who declared the Queen to be allergic to her courtiers, to her own children, to the King himself.

But at least life went forward. Acts of proclamation. The Admiral's Ball, already mentioned. And the Spring Rites on the royal parade grounds where the Queen could be glimpsed by one and all, waving her handkerchief, bravely blessing her subjects with the emblem of her disability. People are fed by that kind of example. Yes, they are. People find courage in stubborn endurance.

But recently the Queen has disappeared, and matters have suddenly worsened. There has been an official announcement that clocks and calendars are to be destroyed. It is forbidden now to utter the names of the days and months, to speak of yesterday or tomorrow or next week. Naturally there will be no Spring Rites this year, for the progression of seasons has been declared unlawful. Meteorologists have been dismissed from their positions and weather disallowed. The cause of Her Majesty's affliction has been identified. It has been verified absolutely. It seems the measured substance that pushes the world this way and that, the invented sequentiality that hovers between the simple raising and lowering of a teacup, can no longer be tolerated by the Queen.

At last the people understand why the palace windows have been closed up. The temporal movement of the sun and stars must be blocked from her view. Rhythmic pulsations of light threaten her existence, suggesting as they do the unstoppable equation that attaches to mass and energy. She lives in the dark now, blindfolded, in fact. Her ears too have been covered over for fear she will hear the cries of birds, a cock at dawn, a swallow, or an owl hooting its signature on the night sky. She no longer speaks or thinks, since the positioning of noun and verb, of premise and conclusion, demands a progression that invites that toxic essence, that mystery.

But they have overlooked her heart, her poor beating queenly heart. Like a mindless machine it continues to add and subtract. A whimsical toy, it beeps and sighs, singing and songing along the jointed channels of her blood. Counting, counting. Now diminishing. Now swelling. Insisting on its literal dance. Tick-tock, tick-tock. Filling up with deadly arithmetic.

Mirrors

———

WHEN HE THINKS about the people he's known in his life, a good many of them seem to have cultivated some curious strand of asceticism, contrived some gesture of renunciation. They give up sugar. Or meat. Or newspapers. Or neckties. They sell their second car or disconnect the television. They might make a point of staying at home on Sunday evenings or abjuring chemical sprays. Something, anyway, that signals dissent and cuts across the beating heart of their circumstances, reminding them of their other, leaner selves. Their better selves.

He and his wife have claimed their small territory of sacrifice too. For years they've become "known" among their friends for the particular deprivation they've assigned themselves: for the fact that there are no mirrors in their summer house. None at all. None are allowed.

The need to observe ourselves is sewn into us, everyone knows this, but he and his wife have turned their backs on this need, said no to it, at least for the duration of the summer months. Otherwise, they are not very different from other couples nearing the end of middle age—he being sixty, she fifty-eight, their children grown up and married and living hundreds of miles away.

In September they will have been married thirty-five years, and they're already planning a week in New York to celebrate this milestone, five nights at the Algonquin (for sentimental reasons) and a few off-Broadway shows, already booked. They stay away from the big musicals as a rule, preferring, for want of a better word, *serious* drama. Nothing experimental, no drugged angst or scalding discourse, but plays that coolly examine the psychological positioning of men and women in our century. This torn, perplexing century. Men and women who resemble themselves.

They would be disinclined to discuss between them how they've arrived at these harmonious choices in the matter of playgoing, how they are both a little proud, in fact, of their taste for serious drama, proud in the biblical *pride* sense. Just as they're a little proud of their mirrorless summer house on the shores of Big Circle Lake.

Their political views tend to fall in the middle of the spectrum. Financially, you might describe them as medium well off, certainly not wealthy. He has retired, one week ago as a matter of fact, from his own management consulting firm, and she is, has always been, a housewife and active community volunteer. These days she wears a large stylish head of stiffened hair, and he, with no visible regret, is going neatly bald at the forehead and crown.

Walking away from their cottage on Big Circle Lake, you would have a hard time describing its contents or atmosphere: faded colours and pleasing shapes that beg you to stay, to make yourself comfortable. These inviting surfaces slip from remembrance the minute you turn your back. But you would very probably bear in mind their single act of forfeiture: there are no mirrors.

Check the medicine cabinet in the little fir-panelled bathroom: nothing. Check the back of the broom cupboard door in the kitchen or the spot above the dresser in their large skylighted bedroom or the wall over the log-burning fireplace in what they choose to call "the lounge." Even if you were to abuse the rules of privacy and look into her (the wife's) big canvas handbag you would find nothing compromising. You would likely come across a compact of face powder, Elizabeth Arden, but the little round mirror lining most women's compacts has been removed. You can just make out the curved crust of glue that once held a mirror in place.

Check even the saucepans hanging over the kitchen stove. Their bottoms are discoloured copper, scratched aluminum. No chance for a reflective glimpse there. The stove itself is dull textured, ancient.

This mirrorlessness of theirs is deliberate, that much is clear.

From June to August they choose to forget who they are, or at least what they look like, electing an annual season of non-reflectiveness in the same way other people put away their clocks for the summer or their computers or door keys or microwave ovens.

"But how can you possibly shave?" people ask the husband, knowing he is meticulous about such things.

He moves a hand to his chin. At sixty, still slender, he remains a handsome man. "By feel," he says. He demonstrates, moving the forefinger of his left hand half an inch ahead of the path of an imaginary razor. "Just try it. Shut your eyes and you'll see you can manage a decent shave without the slightest difficulty. Maybe not a perfect shave, but good enough for out at the lake."

His wife, who never was slender, who has fretted for the better part of her life about her lack of slenderness—raged and grieved, gained and lost—has now at fifty-eight given up the battle. She looks forward to her mirrorless summers, she says. She likes to tell her friends—and she and her husband are a fortunate couple with a large circle of friends—that she can climb into her swimsuit and walk through the length of the cottage—the three original rooms, the new south-facing wing—without having to look even once at the double and triple pinches of flesh that have accumulated in those corners where her shoulders and breasts flow together. "Oh, I suppose I could look down and *see* what I'm like," she says, rolling her eyes, "but I'm not obliged to take in the whole panorama every single day."

She does her hair in the morning in much the same way her husband shaves: by feel, brushing it out, patting it into shape, fixing it with pins. She's been putting on earrings for forty years, and certainly doesn't require a mirror for that. As for lipstick, she makes do with a quick crayoning back and forth across her mouth, a haphazard double slash of colour. Afterwards she returns the lipstick smartly to its case, then runs a practised finger around her upper and lower lips, which she stretches wide so that the shaping of pale raspberry fits perfectly the face she knows by heart.

He's watched her perform this small act a thousand times, so often that his own mouth sometimes wants to stretch in response.

They were newly married and still childless when they bought the cottage, paying far too much, then discovering almost immediately the foundations were half rotted, and carpenter ants—or something—lived in the pine rafters. Mice had made a meal of the electric wires; ants thronged the mildewed cupboards. Officially the place had been sold to them furnished, but the previous owners had taken the best of what there was, leaving only a sagging couch, a table that sat unevenly on the torn linoleum, two battered chairs, a bed with a damp mattress, and an oak dresser with a stuck drawer. The dresser was the old-fashioned kind with its own mirror frame attached, two curving prongs rising gracefully like a pair of arms, but the mirror it had once embraced was missing.

You would think the larceny of the original owners would have embittered the two of them. Or that the smell of mould and rot and accumulated dirt would have filled them with discouragement, but it didn't. They set to work. For three weeks they worked from morning to dusk.

First he repaired the old pump so they might at least have water. He was not in those years adept with his hands, and the task took several days. During that period he washed himself in the lake, not taking the time for a swim, but stopping only to splash his face and body with cold water. She noticed there was a three-cornered smudge of dirt high on his forehead that he missed. It remained there for several days, making him appear to her boyish and vulnerable. She didn't have the heart to mention it to him. In fact, she felt a small ping of sorrow when she looked up at him one evening and found it washed away. Even though she was not in those days an impulsive woman, she had stretched herself forward and kissed the place where the smudge had been.

Curiously, he remembers her spontaneous kiss, remembers she had washed her hair in the lake a few minutes earlier, and had wrapped a towel around her head like a turban. She was not a vain woman. In fact, she had always mourned too much the failures of her body, and so he knew she had no idea of how seductive she looked at that moment with the added inch of towelling and her face bared like a smooth shell.

At night they fell exhausted into the old bed and slept as though weights were attached to their arms and legs. Their completed tasks, mending and painting, airing and polishing, brought them a brimming level of satisfaction that would have been foolish to try to explain to anyone else. They stepped carefully across their washed floorboards, opened and shut their windows and seemed to be listening at night to the underhum of the sloping, leaking roof. That first summer they scarcely saw a soul. The northern shore of Big Circle Lake was a wilderness in those days. There were no visitors, few interruptions. Two or three times they went to town for groceries. Once they attended a local auction and bought a pine bed, a small table, and a few other oddments. Both of them remember they looked carefully for a mirror, but none was to their liking. It was then they decided to do without.

Each day they spent at the cottage became a plotted line, the same coffee mugs (hers, his), the comically inadequate paring knife and the comments that accrued around it. Familiar dust, a pet spider swaying over their bed, the sky lifting and falling and spreading out like a mesh of silver on the lake. Meals. Sleep. A surprising amount of silence.

They thought they'd known each other before they married. He'd reported dutifully, as young men were encouraged to do in those days, his youthful experiences and pleasures, and she, blocked with doubt, had listed off hers. The truth had been darkened out. Now it erupted, came to the surface. He felt a longing to turn to her and say: "This is what I've dreamed of all my life, being this tired, this used up, and having someone like you, exactly like you, waking up at my side."

At the end of that first married summer they celebrated with dinner at a restaurant at the far end of the lake, the sort of jerry-built knotty-pine family establishment that opens in May for the summer visitors and closes on Labour Day. The waitresses were students hired for the season, young girls wearing fresh white peasant blouses and gathered skirts and thonged sandals on their feet. These girls, holding their trays sideways, manoeuvred through the warren of tiny rooms. They brought chilled tomato juice, set a basket of bread on the table, put mixed salad out in wooden bowls, then swung back into the kitchen for plates of chicken and vegetables. Their rhythmic ease, burnished to perfection now that summer was near its end, was infectious, and the food, which was really no better than such food can be, became a meal each of them would remember with pleasure.

He ate hungrily. She cut more slowly into her roast

chicken, then looked up, straight into what she at first thought was a window. In fact, it was a mirror that had been mounted on the wall, put there no doubt to make the cramped space seem larger. She saw a woman prettier than she remembered, a graceful woman, deeply tanned, her eyes lively, the shoulders moving sensually under her cotton blouse. A moment ago she had felt a pinprick of envy for the lithe careless bodies of the young waitresses. Now she was confronted by this stranger. She opened her mouth as if to say: who on earth?

She'd heard of people who moved to foreign countries and forgot their own language, the simplest words lost: door, tree, sky. But to forget your own face? She smiled; her face smiled back; the delay of recognition felt like treasure. She put down her knife and fork and lifted her wrists forward in a salute.

Her husband turned then and looked into the mirror. He too seemed surprised. "Hello," he said fondly. "Hello, us."

Their children were six and eight the year they put the addition on the cottage. Workmen came every morning, and the sound of their power tools shattered the accustomed summer-time peace. She found herself living all day for the moment they would be gone, the sudden late-afternoon stillness and the delicious green smell of cut lumber rising around them. The children drifted through the half-completed partitions like ghosts, claiming their own territory. For two nights, while the new roof was being put on, they slept with their beds facing straight up to the stars.

That was the year her daughter came running into the kitchen in a new swimsuit, asking where the mirror was. Her tone was excited but baffled, and she put her hands over her mouth as though she knew she had blundered somehow just presenting this question.

"We don't have a mirror at the cottage," her mother explained.

"Oh," the child replied. Just "Oh."

At that moment the mother remembered something she had almost forgotten. In the old days, when a woman bought a new purse, or a pocketbook as they were called then, it came packed hard with grey tissue paper. And in the midst of all the paper wadding there was always a little unframed rectangle of mirror. These were crude, roughly made mirrors, and she wasn't sure that people actually used them. They were like charms, good-luck charms. Or like compasses; you could look in them and take your bearings. Locate yourself in the world.

We use the expression "look *into* a mirror," as though it were an open medium, like water—which the first mirrors undoubtedly were. Think of Narcissus. He started it all. And yet it is women who are usually associated with mirrors:

Mermaids rising up from the salty waves with a comb and a mirror in hand. Cleopatra on her barge. Women and vanity went hand in hand.

In his late forties he fell in love with another woman. Was she younger than his wife? Yes, of course she was younger. She was more beautiful too, though with a kind of beauty that had to be checked and affirmed almost continually. Eventually it wore him out.

He felt he had only narrowly escaped. He had broken free, and by a mixture of stealth and good fortune had kept his wife from knowing. Arriving that summer at the house on Big Circle Lake, he turned the key rather creakily in the door. His wife danced through ahead of him and did a sort of triple turn on the kitchen floor, a dip-shuffle-dip, her arms extended, her fingers clicking imaginary castanets. She always felt lighter at the lake, her body looser. This lightness, this proof of innocence, doubled his guilt. A wave of darkness had rolled in between what he used to be and what he'd become, and he longed to put his head down on the smooth pine surface of the kitchen table and confess everything.

Already his wife was unpacking a box of groceries, humming as she put things away. Oblivious.

There was one comfort, he told himself: for two months there would be no mirrors to look into. His shame had made him unrecognizable anyway.

He spent the summer building a cedar deck, which he

knew was the sort of thing other men have done in such circumstances.

She had always found it curious that mirrors, which seemed magical in their properties, in their ability to multiply images and augment light, were composed of only two primary materials: a plane of glass pressed up against a plane of silver. Wasn't there something more required? Was this really all there was to it?

The simplicity of glass. The preciousness of silver. Only these two elements were needed for the miracle of reflection to take place. When a mirror was broken, the glass could be replaced. When a mirror grew old, it had only to be resilvered. There was no end to a mirror. It could go on and on. It could go on forever.

Perhaps her life was not as complicated as she thought. Her concerns, her nightmares, her regrets, her suspicions—perhaps everything would eventually be repaired, healed, obliterated. Probably her husband was right: she made too much of things.

"You remind me of someone," she said the first time they met. He knew she meant that he reminded her of herself. Some twinned current flowed between them. This was years and years ago.

But her words came back to him recently when his children and their families were visiting at Big Circle Lake.

The marriages of his son and daughter are still young, still careful, often on the edge of hurt feelings or quarrels, though he feels fairly certain they will work their way eventually towards a more even footing, whatever that means.

He's heard it said all his life that the young pity the old, that this pity is a fact of human nature. But he can't help observing how both his grown children regard him with envy. They almost sigh it out—"You've got everything."

Well, it's so. His mortgage is paid. There's this beautiful place for the summer. Time to travel now. Old friends. A long marriage. A bank of traditions. He imagines his son and daughter must amuse their separate friends with accounts of their parents' voluntary forswearing of mirrors, and that in these accounts he and his wife are depicted as harmless eccentrics who have perhaps stumbled on some useful verity which has served to steady them in their lives.

He longs sometimes to tell them that what they see is not the whole of it. Living without mirrors is cumbersome and inconvenient, if the truth were known, and, moreover, he has developed a distaste in recent years for acts of abnegation, finding something theatrical and childish about cultivated denial, something stubbornly wilful and self-cherishing.

He would also like to tell them that other people's lives are seldom as settled as they appear. That every hour contains at least a moment of bewilderment or worse. That a whim randomly adopted grows forlorn with time, and that people who have lived together for thirty-five years still apprehend each other as strangers.

Though only last night—or was it the night before—he woke suddenly at three in the morning and found his wife had turned on her light and was reading. He lay quiet, watching her for what seemed like several minutes: a woman no longer young, intent on her book, lifting a hand every moment or two to turn over a page, her profile washed out by the high-intensity lamp, her shoulders and body blunted by shadow. Who was this person?

And then she had turned and glanced his way. Their eyes held, caught on the thread of a shared joke: the two of them at this moment had become each other, at home behind the screen of each other's face. It was several seconds before he was able to look away.

The Harp

———

THE HARP WAS FALLING through the air, only I didn't know it was a harp. It was only this blocky chunk of matter, vaguely triangular, this *thing*, silhouetted against the city sky, held there for a split second like a stencil's hard-edged blank, more of an absence than a real object of heft and substance. It threw off a single glint of gold as it spun downward, I remembered that afterwards.

Everyone stopped and stared, which is surprising in a city this size, and especially at that hour, the end of the workday, and people hurrying home or stopping to do a little last-minute Christmas shopping. Yesterday's fall of snow was fast turning to urban slush. I remember thinking how oddly comforting the cold slush felt against the side of my face and along the exposed part of my leg, a sort of anaesthetic or sensory diversion. My own father, when seized by shoulder cramps last spring, had favoured ice packs over a hot-water bottle, and this was one more thing he and my mother quarrelled about. That long list made up their life together. Leisure, food, work, housing, the sentient pleas-ures, the hour of bedtime, tea versus hot chocolate, heat versus cold; they agree on nothing.

Someone near me let out a shriek, there were scuffling sounds as I went down hard on the pavement, and then a sudden closed silence as people in their overcoats crowded around me. I blinked and saw a man stoop and put his gloved hand on my bare leg. My pantyhose; what had happened to my pantyhose?—a brand new pair put on earlier in the day. "You're going to be fine," he said, and someone else pronounced the word "harp," that puzzling little word leaping out of a strand of other, less audible words.

It seems—yes, it was true—I had been struck on my left leg by the wood post of a large concert harp falling from an overhead window, and this smashed instrument lay next to me now in the soft grey slush, two inert bodies side by side. It and me. Fallen sisters. A streetlight shone overhead. I flung out a hand and, with more reflex than intention, struck violently against the harp's strings, and was rewarded by a musical growl, very low in tone and with the merest suggestion of vibrato. The crowd around me applauded. What could they have been thinking? That I, wounded on the street, ambushed, had decided to perform an impromptu concert? "There, there," one of them said, "the ambulance is coming."

Explanations followed, although there are no explanations that quite cover this kind of random accident. There had been a Christmas party on the second floor of the Blair Building, a gathering of accountants and their spouses standing about drinking spiced wine and eating little hot rolled-up tidbits of bacon and cheese, and one of the more bibulous guests had stumbled against the harpist—it was said by someone that he had been flirting openly with her—and knocked the instrument against the window, which immediately shattered.

"What a good thing you were hit by the harp and not the glass," people said. "How fortunate you were to be struck on the leg and not the head," others offered. I cried for two days, drenching my hospital sheets with my tears, weeping from the shock and the pain and the stupidity of people's remarks, and also because I had not been invited to the accountants' party, never mind that I am not an accountant myself or acquainted with one.

Was there any justice in the world? Think about it. Why should I have been shivering along on a dark slush-strewn street when I might have been standing aloft in that warm, crowded, scented room, reaching for one more pastry puff, one more glass of fragrant wine, and taking in, as though it were my right, the soft background tinkling of harp music; my name printed on the invitation list, part of the ongoing celebration of the season.

X-rays were taken, of course, and it was determined that a chip of bone had broken away from my left shin. Nothing could be done about this detached piece of tissue, I was going to have to live my life without it, just as I have learned to accommodate other subtractions. The bruising would disappear in a week or so. Painkillers were prescribed. A counsellor arrived to help me deal with trauma, and the chaplain enjoined me to give thanks for having been spared even greater injury. The newspapers requested interviews, but these I resisted.

I phoned my mother in Calgary. ("You always were clumsy," she said.) And my father in Montana. (Did I mention that my parents have decided to separate after all these years?) He, with his hearing impairment, came away from our conversation believing I had been struck not by a harp but by a heart. "That doesn't sound too serious to me," he said in his fatherly way. "A heart is a relatively soft and buoyant organ." And then he said, "You'll get over it in no time."

The harpist visited me in the hospital. Her body was tense. Her face was red. She kept her coat on, buttoned up, during the whole of the visit. The harp was being examined by experts. It might be repairable or it might not, but in any case the expense was going to be exorbitant—and here was she, without insurance, and for the time being without any means of earning a living. It seemed only reasonable, she said, that I contribute to her costs.

Only my dreams are benign. In these nightly visitations the harp is not plummeting but floating. The December air presses on its gilded strings tenderly, with the greatest tact, and I am transformed, unrehearsed, into the guest of honour, awarded the unexpected buoyancy of flight itself, as I reach out to catch the whole of my life in my arms.

Our Men
and Women

—

OUR EARTHQUAKE MAN is up early. He greets the soft dawn with a speculative lift of his orange-juice glass. "Hello, little earth," he hums quietly. Then, "So! You're still here."

He puts in a pre-breakfast call to the E-Quake Centre. "Nothing much," he hears. "Just a few overnight rumbles."

Overnight what? Really?

He resents having missed these terrestrial waves, but his resentment is so faint, so almost non-existent, he swallows it down, along with his vitamin C. He should be grateful. So he's missed a tremble or two! What does it matter?—the earth is always heaving, growling, whereas last night he'd slept seven uninterrupted hours with his arms and legs wrapped around the body of his dear Patricia, his blond Patricia, graceful, lithe Patricia, fifteen years his junior, blessed replacement for Marguerite—perpetrator of sulks, rages, the hurling of hairbrushes and dinner plates. Thirty-five years he and Marguerite were together. Their four grown children are almost embarrassingly buoyant about this second marriage of his. At the time of the wedding, last Thanksgiving, two days after a 3.5 Richter-scale reading, the kids chipped in together to buy their old dad and his new wife an antique sleigh bed. Actually a reproduction model, produced in a North Carolina factory. Sleek, beautiful. Closer in its configuration to a cradle than a sleigh.

Now, in the early morning, Patricia is grilling slices of seven-grain bread over the backyard barbecue. She has a thing about toasters, just as he has a thing about the instability of the earth. You'd think he'd be used to it after all this time, but his night dreams are of molten lava, and the crunch and grind of tectonic plates. As a graduate student he believed his subtle calibrations could predict disaster; now he knows better. Those years with Marguerite taught him that making projections is like doing push-ups in water. The world spewed and shifted. There was nothing to lean against. You had to pull yourself back from it, suck in your gut, and hold still.

His solemn, smiling Patricia is flipping over the toast now with a long silvery fork. Sunlight decorates her whisked-back hair and the rounded cotton shoulder of her T-shirt. What a picture! She stands balanced with her bare feet slightly apart on the patio stones, defying—it would seem—the twitching earth with its sly, capricious crust. "Ready?" she calls out to him, skewering the slices of toast on her fork and tossing them straight at his head.

But no. It's only an optical illusion. The toast is still there, attached to the fork's prongs. It's a hug she's thrown in his direction. Her two skinny arms have risen exuberantly, grabbed a broad cube of air, and pushed it forcefully towards him.

It came at him, a tidal wave moving along a predestined line. This is what his nightmares have promised: disorder, violence.

A man of reflexes, his first thought was to duck, to cover his face and protect himself. Then he remembered who he was, where he was—a man standing in a sunlit garden a few yards away from a woman he loved. He can't quite, yet, believe this. "Tsunami," he pronounced speculatively.

"Me too," she whispered. "Hey, me too."

Our Rainfall woman is also up early. She parts her dotted-Swiss curtains and inspects the sky. Good, fine, okay; check. A smack of blue, like an empty billboard, fills in the spaces behind her flowering shrubs and cedar fence; she finds this reassuring, also disappointing. Her whole day will be like this, a rocking back and forth between what she wants and what she doesn't. "I am master of all I can stand," her father, the great explainer, used to say. She can't remember if he meant this thought to be comforting or if he was being his usual arrogant, elliptical self.

At eleven o'clock she conducts her seminar on drought. At four-thirty she's scheduled to lecture on flood. Lunch will be a sandwich and a pot of tea in the staff room. They expect her to be there. Today someone asks her about the World Series, who she's betting on. "Hmmmm," she says, blinking, looking upwards, moving her mug of tea swiftly to her lips. Then, "Hard to say, hard to say."

Her night dreams, her day-dreams too, are about drowning, but in recent months she's been enrolled in an evening workshop at the Y that teaches new techniques guaranteed to control nocturnal disturbances. It works like this: In the midst of sleep, the conscious mind is invited to step forward and engage briefly with the dream image, so that a threatening wave of water closing over the dreamer's head (for example) is transformed into a shower of daisies. Or soap flakes. Or goose feathers. An alternative strategy is to bid the conscious mind to reach for the remote control (so to speak) and switch channels. Even her father's flat elderly argumentative voice can be shut off. Right off, snap, click. Or transmuted into a trill of birdsong. Or the dappled pattern of light and shadow.

She lives, by choice, in a part of the country where rain is moderate. There's never too much or too little. Except—

well, except during exceptional circumstances, which could occur next week or next month, anytime, in fact. Planetary systems are enormously complicated; they tend to interact erratically. She understands this, having written any number of articles on the very subject of climate variability, on the theory of chaos. Meteorologists, deservedly humbled in recent years, confess that they are working *towards* eighty-five percent accuracy, and that this thrust applies only to twenty-four-hour predictions. Long-term forecasting, the darling of her graduate school days, has been abandoned.

There's no way people can protect themselves against surprise. Her father, for instance, was one minute alive and the next minute dead. The space in between was so tightly packed that there wasn't room to squeeze in one word.

Our Fire fellow is relatively young, but already he's been granted tenure. Also five thousand square feet of laboratory space, plus three research assistants, plus an unlimited travel allowance. Anything he wants he gets, and he wants a lot. He's gassed up on his own brilliance. And with shame too. No one should need what he needs, and need it ten times a day, a hundred times a day.

He's a man of finely gauged increments, of flashpoints, of fevers and starbursts, of a rich unsparing cynicism. Up at five-thirty, a four-mile run, a quick flick through the latest journals, half a dozen serious articles gulped down, then coffee, scalding, out of a machine. This part of the day is a torment to him, his night dreams still not shaken off. (Has it been made clear that he lives by choice in a motel unit, and refuses even the consolation of weekly rates?)

By seven he's in his office, checking through his E-mail, firing off letters which become quarrels or sharp inquiries. Everywhere he sees slackers, defilers, and stumblers. His anger blazes just thinking of them. He knows he should exercise patience, but fear of anonymity, or something equally encumbering, has edged the sense of risk out of his life.

Small talk, small courtesies—he hasn't time. His exigent nature demands instant responses and deplores time-wasting functions. Like what? Like that wine-and-cheese reception for old What's-His-Name and his new wife! Like staff-room niceties. Blather about the World Series. And that lachrymose young Rainfall woman who keeps asking him how he's "getting along."

Well, he's getting along. And along and along. He's going up, up. Up like a firecracker.

Right now he's doing fifty double-time push-ups on the beige carpet of his office in preparation for one of his popular lectures on reality. His premise, briefly, is that we can only touch reality through the sensations of the single moment, that infinitesimal spark of time which is, even now as we consider it, dying. We must—to use his metaphor—place our hand directly in the flame.

He pursues his point, romping straight over the usual

curved hills of faith, throwing forth a stupefying mixture of historical lore and its gossamer logic, presenting arguments that are bejewelled with crafty irrelevance, covering the blackboard with many-branched equations that establish and illuminate his careful, random proofs. On and on he goes, burning dangerously bright, and ever brighter.

Notes are taken. No one interrupts, no one poses questions, they wouldn't dare. Afterwards the lecture hall empties quickly, leaving him alone on the podium, steaming with his own heat, panting, rejoicing.

But grief steals into his nightly dreams, which commence with a vision of drenching rain, rain that goes on and on and shows no sign of ever ending, falling into the rooms of his remembered boyhood, his mother, his father—there they are, smiling, so full of parental pride— and a brother, especially a brother, who is older, stronger, more given to acts of shrugging surrender, more self-possessed, more eagerly and more offhandedly anointed. The family's clothes and bodies are soaked through with rain, as are the green hedges, the familiar woods and fields, the roadway, the glistening roofs and chimneys, inclines and valleys, the whole world, in fact. Except for him, standing there with his hands cupped, waiting. For him there has not been, so far, a single drop.

She's something else, our Plague and Pestilence woman. She's just (today) won the staff-room World Series pool—

a lucky guess, she admits, the first four games out of seven. No one else risked such a perfect sky-blue sweep.

"You were an accident," her mother told her when she was a young girl, just ten or eleven years old. "I never meant to have a kid, it just happened. There I was, pregnant."

Unforgivable words. But instantly forgiven. Because her mother's voice, as she made this confession, was roughened with wonder. An accident, she said, but her intonation, her slowly shaking woman's head, declared it to be the best accident imaginable. The most fortunate event in the history of the world, no less.

Our Plague and Pestilence woman married young, out of love, a man who was selfish, moody, cruel, childish. But one day, several years into the marriage, he woke up and thought, "I can't go on like this. I have to change. I have to become a different kind of person."

They are thankful, both of them, that their children have been spared the ravages of smallpox, typhoid, diphtheria, scarlet fever, poliomyelitis. Other diseases, worse diseases, hover about them, but the parents remain hopeful. Their histories, their natural inclinations, buoy them up. She dreams nightly of leaf mould, wheat rot, toads falling from the sky, multiplying bacteria, poisoned blood, incomprehensible delusions, but wakes up early each day with a clean sharp longing for simple tasks and agreeable weather.

It was our Plague and Pestilence woman who, one year ago, introduced her assistant, Patricia, to the recently widowed Earthquake man, and this matchmaking success has inspired another social occasion—which occurred just last night, as a matter of fact. A platter of chicken, shrimp, saffron, and rice was prepared. A table was set in a shaded garden. The two guests—our Rainfall woman, our Fire person—were reluctant at first to come. They had to be persuaded, entreated. Once there, they were put, more or less, at their ease. Made to feel they deserved the fragrant dish before them. Invited to accept whatever it was that poured through their senses. Encouraged to see that the image they glimpsed in the steady candlelight matched almost, but not quite, the shapeless void of their private nightly dreams.

Our P and P woman, observant as she is, doesn't yet know how any of this will turn out. It's far too soon to tell.

We can't help being proud of our men and women. They work hard to understand the topography of the real. It's a heartbreaking struggle, yet somehow they carry on—predicting, measuring, analysing, recording, looking over their shoulders at the presence of their accumulated labour, cocking an ear to the sounds of their alarm clocks going off and calling them to temperature-controlled rooms and the dings and dongs of their word processors, the shrill bells of approval or disapproval, the creaks of their bodies as the years pile up, and the never-ending quarrel with their smothered, creaturely, solitary selves. Limitations—always they're crowded up against limitations. Sometimes our men and women give way to old nightmares or denial or the delusion that living in the world is effortless and full of ease. Like everyone else, they're spooked by old injuries, and that swift plummeting fall towards what they believe must be the future. Nevertheless they continue to launch their various theories, theories so fragile, speculative, and foolish, so unanchored by proofs and possibilities, and so distorted by their own yearnings, that their professional reputations are put at risk, their whole lives, you might say. Occasionally, not often, they are called upon to commit an act of extraordinary courage.

Which is why we stand by our men and women. In the end they may do nothing. In the meantime, they do what they can.

Keys

BIFF MONKHOUSE, the man who brought bebop to Europe, collapsed and died last week in the lobby of the George V Hotel in Paris. His was a life full of success and failure, full of love and the absence of love. The famous "teddy boy" attire he affected was a kind of self-advertisement saying: I am outside of time and nationality, beyond gender and class.

No wallet or passport was found on his person.

No coins, snapshots, receipts, letters, or lists were found on his person.

No spectacles, prescriptions, pills, phone numbers, credit cards were found on his person.

No rings, wrist-watches, chains, tattoos, or distinguishing scars were found on his person.

No alcohol, caffeine, heroin, crack, or HIV-positive cells were found in his bloodstream.

No odour attached to his body.

His hair had been recently cut. His nails were pared, his shoes only lightly scuffed. His right hand was closed in a tight fist.

An ambulance attendant pried open Biff Monkhouse's fist half an hour after the collapse and found there, warm and somewhat oily, a plain steel key-ring holding nine keys of various shapes and sizes.

Dr. Marianne Moriarty of Agassiz University read the Biff Monkhouse news item (Reuters) and found it not at all surprising. She's evolved her own complex theory about keys, why people cling to them, what they represent. Every time you turn a key in a lock you make a new beginning—that's one of her beliefs. Keys are useful, portable, and highly metaphorical, suggesting as they do the two postures we most often find ourselves in for either we are locked in…or locked out. In her 1987 doctoral thesis she reported the startling fact that North Americans carry, on average, 5.3 keys. (Those who are prudent have copies hidden away, occasionally in places they no longer remember.) She herself carries twelve keys—condo, office, mailbox, garage, jewelry box, and the like, also a hotel key (Hawaii) she can't bear to send back. Using an approved statistical sample, she's worked out the correlation between the number of keys carried and the educational or economic or age level of the key carrier. Her mother Elsie, for instance, a sixty-six-year-old housewife in the small town of Grindley, Saskatchewan, carries only three keys—back door, front door, safe-deposit box, period—while Marianne's lover, Malcolm Loring, professor emeritus of the Sociology Department, a married man with a private income, carries sixteen keys, one of which unlocks the door of a boathouse that burned down two years ago.

Arson was suspected, but never proven. Sixteen-year-old Christopher MacFarlane, skinny, ponytailed, bad skin, a gaping, shredded hole in the left knee of his blue jeans, and a single unattached, unidentified key in his back pocket, happened to be in the vicinity at the time of the fire. He was questioned, but later released after a somewhat rougher-than-usual body search. The young police sergeant eyed him closely and said, "We'd like you to tell us, sonny, exactly what this key is you've got in your pocket." "I don't know," the boy replied.

He had found the little key in the grass behind the marina. He'd been lying there flat on his belly, running the palm of his hand back and forth across the dry, colourless, shaven blades, feeling the unbreathable heat and thinking about sex—the fundamental circularity of sexual awakening, first longing, then intention and discharge, then satisfaction, and finally quiescence. What was the use of it, he wondered, this wasteful closed rhythm that presented itself again and again like an old fable that wheezes out its endless repetition. It wore away at him. He kept hoping to drive it away, but a kind of anxiety was forever regrowing around his heart, and he felt he would never be free.

And then he saw something burning in the grass near his head, a coin or a bottle cap. But no—when he reached out he found it was a key. It lay lightly in his hand, small and almost weightless, rounded at its head and punched with a ridged hole. The other end—the business end, as some people call it—was dull-toothed, cheaply made, stamped out rather than cut; possibly it was a bicycle key or the key to a locker. Or else—and he pushed himself up on one elbow, peering at it closely, turning it over in his hand—or else it was the key to money or mystery or fame or passion. He slid the little key into his back pocket, where it remained for several weeks, long enough for its silhouette to leave an imprint on the faded denim material, a thready raised patch of white shading off into blue.

The key was later discovered in the dryer of the Harbour Heights Laundromat by one of its regular clients, Cheryl Spence, thirty-four, who lives on the fourteenth floor of a high-rise across the street. It was a Saturday morning. She dumped in her blouses, her full cotton skirts and sundresses, her socks and underwear, her pillowcase and duvet cover. She turns all these items inside out when she launders them, giving them a hard shake as her mother had done, as her grandmother once did, and then she examines the pockets for stray tissues and paper clips. Buttons are buttoned and zippers zipped. She checks the temperature setting, measures the detergent in the little Styrofoam cup provided by the management.

Oh, how orderly and careful I am, she says to herself, how *good*! In her change purse there are plenty of quarters to feed the machines, little silvery stacks of them lying on their sides, rubbing solidly together. If other people doing their laundry on a Saturday morning run short of change, Cheryl can always help them out. Whenever this happens she reflects on what a kind, generous, and altruistic person she is, and what a pity there aren't more good-hearted people in the world like herself. She thinks this, but doesn't say it. As a very young child, not more than six or seven years of age, she understood that she was scheduled to have a double existence—an open life in which her actions were plainly visible, and a hidden life where thought and intention squatted darkly. This powerful separation seems wholly natural to her, not a thing to rage against or even to question. The real world, of course, is in her own head, which she sometimes thinks of as a shut room provisioned with declaration and clarity, everything else being a form of theatre.

The little key she found at the Harbour Heights Laundromat was bent from being tossed about in the dryer's drum. Some of its particularity had been rubbed away by heat and friction. She straightened it as best she could between her fingers, dropped it into her purse, and carried it home. Who knows when she might be confronted by a lock she can't open?

For several months it sat, or rather lay, in a kitchen drawer, in a cracked teacup to be precise, along with a single hairpin, a handful of thumbtacks, a stub of a candle, half an eraser, a blackened French coin, a book of matches from the Infomatic Centre, a rubber band or two, and a few paper clips. Odds and ends. Flotsam and jetsam.

In the evenings, tired out from a day at the accounts office, she likes to read long romantic novels and listen to music on her CD player. One night—it was in the middle of January, in the middle of an ice storm—she sat reading a book called *The Sands of Desire* and listening to a concert of soft rock when she felt herself seized by an impulse to purify her life. The way her thighs broadened out as she sat in her chair, the printed words slipping out of focus, the notes of music—their excess and persistence crowded up against her, depriving her for a frightening moment of oxygen. She opened a window and let the icy air come into her apartment, but it was not enough. She grasped a small corduroy cushion and hurled it out the window, observing with satisfaction the way it spun around in the dark air as it descended, a soft little satellite of foam and fabric. Next she threw into the driving phosphorescence a compact disc she had bought on sale only one week earlier, a medley of country ballads, wailing, weak, and jerky with tears. In a kitchen cupboard she found a family-sized package of Cheese Twists, then a brown-edged head of lettuce in the refrigerator—out they went, one after the other, sailing off the tips of her fingers. And finally, in a gesture that was a kind of suicide or ritual cleansing, she didn't know which, she emptied out the cracked china cup with its miserable, broken, mismatched contents, its unsorted detritus of economy and mystery. It seemed to her she could hear the separate items rattling down through the frozen tree branches and landing like a shower of meteorites on the rooftops of the cars parked below—the paper clips, the thumbtacks, the little bent key. Ping. Tut. Tsk, Tick. Gone.

This same Cheryl Spence has visited the Pioneer Museum at Steinbach and the Reptile Museum on Highway 70 and the Wax Museum in Minneapolis, but she has never even heard of the Museum of Keys in the city of Buffalo, that dark old American city of cracked alleys and beef-coloured bricks. A rough place, a tough place—but underlying its rough toughness, buried there like a seam of limestone, is the hoarded and invested money of a dozen or so millionaires no one's ever heard of, men made rich on meat, screws, plastics, textiles, optics, leather, and the like. One of them, a manufacturer of table silver, established the Museum of Keys some years ago as a showcase for his own extensive key collection.

His interest in keys began at the age of sixty, at a time when he was recovering from a serious heart attack. It was

Christmas morning. He was seated in an armchair, a blanket over his knees, ashamed of that soft-fringed covering, ashamed of his cold feet in their slippers and the weak light that drifted in from the east-facing window. His wife presented him with an antique porcelain music box shaped like a shepherdess. Always before she had given him practical, manly objects such as fountain pens or fishing gear. What was he to make of a figurine with flounced china skirts, revolving slowly and playing the same merry waltz tune again and again and again? He sensed some covert meaning in his wife's offering—for there she stood, inches away from him, so rounded, pale-fleshed, and mildly luminous, so timid in her posture and so fragile (with a head that tipped sideways and one hand clasping the pleats of her skirt), though her gaze at the moment of gift-giving was oddly sharpened and sly; she held her breath in her throat as though it were something breakable like ice or glass or part of the solitude she sometimes drew around herself. He loved her, and had never thought of her as a shrewd or demanding woman, yet here she was, waiting to be thanked, that much was clear, to be awarded an explosion of gratitude he had no way of formulating. He was not schooled in such expressions. Tact or shyness had kept him ignorant.

Her name was Anna. He knew, intimately, after thirty years of marriage, the floury cellular creases of her neck and elbows, her breasts, hips, and round, shining ankles; he knew too, or rather sensed, that real intimacy was essentially painful—to those locked in its embrace as much as those shut out. In his confusion, his embarrassment, he seized on the exquisitely fashioned silver key, which at least possessed familiar weight and form.

How beautifully it fit his hand. How concentrated was its purpose. He had only to insert it in the shepherdess's glazed petticoats, that slender place at the back of her waist that has no name, and the mechanism was engaged. A twist or two released a ruffling of bells in triple meter. In the moment before the music began—and this was the part he grew to love best—there could be heard a brief sliding hum of gears shifting into place, anxious to perform, wonderfully obedient to the key's delicate persuasion.

The second key he acquired belonged to the lost oak door, or so he imagines it, of a demolished Breton chapel. It is thirteen inches long, made of black iron, rough in texture but beautifully balanced. "Notice the beautiful balance," he says when showing it off, always employing the same exclamatory phrase and allowing the key to seesaw across the back of his wrist. Some of his other keys—before long there were hundreds—are made of rare alloys; many are highly decorated and set with semiprecious stones, pieces of jade or turquoise. One of the most curious is fifteen hundred years old, Chinese, and another, dating from the days of the Roman Empire, is made so it can be worn on the finger like a little ring. There are keys from the

Middle Ages with elaborate, ingenious warding devices and there is also a small, flat, unprepossessing key—entirely unornamented—which is said to be the prototype of the Yale (or pin tumbler) key invented in Middletown, Connecticut, in the year 1848.

The Museum of Keys is located in the southwest corner of the city, admission free, closed on Mondays, and offering school tours every Tuesday. A portrait of Anna _____, the founder's wife, 1903–1972, hangs on the wall behind the literature display. Ten thousand visitors come through the doors each year, and often they leave the museum jingling their own keys in their pockets or regarding them with new respect, perhaps thinking how strange it is that keys, the most private and secret parts of ourselves, are nevertheless placed under doormats or flowerpots for visiting friends, or hung on a nail at the back of the garage for the gas-meter man, or mailed around the world in padded envelopes, acknowledging in this bitter, guarded century our lapses of attention.

A seven-year-old boy taken along with his class to the museum in Buffalo stares into a display case. His gaze settles on a long, oddly shaped wooden key (Babylonian), and his hand flies instantly to the key he wears around his neck, the key that will let him into his house on North Lilac Avenue after school, one hour before his mother returns from her job at the bottling plant. When first tying the key in place, she had delivered certain warnings: the key must not be lost, lent, or even shown to others, but must be kept buried under his sweater all day long, accompanying him everywhere, protecting him from danger.

He doesn't need protection, not that he could ever explain this to his mother; he knows how to jump and hustle and keep himself watchful. The key leads him home and into a warm hallway, the light switch waiting, a note on the refrigerator, the television set sending him a wide, waxy smile of welcome. There is no danger, none at all; his mother has been misled, her notion of the world somehow damaged. Still, he loves this key (so icy against his skin when he slips it on, but warming quickly to body temperature) and has to restrain himself, whenever he feels restless, from reaching inside his clothes and fingering its edges.

He is a solemn child whose thoughts are full of perforations (how it would feel to bite into a red crayon or put his tongue to the rain-soaked bushes behind the schoolyard fence), or else opening onto a lively boil of fantasy that tends to be dotted with bravery and tribute. And yet, for all his imaginative powers, he cannot—at his age—begin to picture the unscrolling of a future in which he will one day possess a key-ring (in the shape of the Eiffel Tower) which will hold a pair of streamlined rubber-tipped car keys, as well as a rainbow of pale tinted others—house, office, club, cottage—and a time when he will have a curly-headed wife with her own set of keys (on a thong of red leather stamped with her initials) and a fourteen-year-old daughter whose miniature brass key will open a diary in which she will write out her secret thoughts, beneath which lie a secondary drift of thought too tentative, too sacred, too rare to trust to the inexactitude of print and to the guardianship of a mere key.

Absence

———

S HE WOKE UP EARLY, drank a cup of strong unsugared
coffee, then sat down at her word processor. She knew
more or less what she wanted to do, and that was to create
a story that possessed a granddaughter, a Boston fern,
a golden apple, and a small blue cradle. But after she
had typed half a dozen words, she found that one of the
letters of the keyboard was broken, and, to make matters
worse, a vowel, the very letter that attaches to the hungry
self.

Of course she had no money and no house-handy mate
to prod the key free. Many a woman would have shrugged
good-naturedly, conceded defeat, and left the small stones
of thought unclothed, but not our woman; our woman
rolled up her sleeves, to use that thready old metaphor, and
began afresh. She would work *around* the faulty letter. She

would be resourceful, look for other ways, and make an artefact out of absence. She would, to put the matter bluntly, make do.

She started—slowly, ponderously—to tap out words. "Several thousand years ago there—"

But where her hands had once danced, they now trudged. She stopped and scratched her head, her busy, normally useful head, that had begun, suddenly, to thrum and echo; where could she go from here? she asked herself sharply. Because the flabby but dependable gerund had dropped through language's trapdoor, gone. Whole parcels of grammar, for that matter, seemed all at once out of reach, and so were those bulky doorstop words that connect and announce and allow a sentence to pause for a moment and take on fresh loads of oxygen. Vocabulary, her well-loved garden, as broad and taken-for-granted as an acre of goldenrod, had shrunk to a square yard, and she was, as never before, forced to choose her words, much as her adored great-aunt, seated at a tea table, had selected sugar lumps by means of a carefully executed set of tongs.

She was tempted, of course, to seek out synonyms, and who could blame her? But words, she knew, held formal levels of sense and shades of deference that were untransferable one to the other, though thousands of deluded souls hunch each day over crossword puzzles and try. The glue of resonance makes austere demands. Memory barks, and context, that absolute old cow, glowers and chews up what's less than acceptable.

The woman grew, as the day wore on, more and more frustrated. Always the word she sought, the only word, teased and taunted from the top row of the broken keyboard, a word that spun around the centre of a slender, one-legged vowel, erect but humble, whose dot of amazement had never before mattered.

Furthermore, to have to pause and pry an obscure phrase from the dusty pages of her old thesaurus threw her off balance and altered the melody of her prose. Between stutters and starts, the sheen was somehow lost; the small watery pleasures of accent and stress were roughened up as though translated from some coarse sub-Balkan folk tale and rammed through the nozzle of a too-clever-by-half, space-larky computer.

Her head-bone ached; her arm-bones froze; she wanted only to make, as she had done before, sentences that melted at the centre and branched at the ends, that threatened to grow unruly and run away, but that clause for clause adhered to one another as though stuck down by Velcro tabs.

She suffered too over the *sounds* that evaded her and was forced to settle for those other, less seemly vowels whose open mouths and unsubtle throats yawned and groaned and showed altogether too much teeth. She preferred small slanted breakable tones that scarcely made themselves known unless you pressed an ear closely to the

curled end of the tongue or the spout of a kettle. The
thump of heartbeat was what she wanted, but also the small
urgent jumps lodged between the beats. (She was thankful,
though, for the sly *y* that now and then leapt forward and
pulled a sentence taut as a cord.)

"Several thousand years ago a woman sat down at a
table and began to—"

Hours passed, but the work went badly. She thought
to herself: to make a pot of bean soup would produce
more pleasure. To vacuum the hall rug would be of
more use.

Both sense and grace eluded her, but hardest to bear
was the fact that the broken key seemed to demand of her
a parallel surrender, a correspondence of economy sub-
tracted from the alphabet of her very self. But how? A story
had to come from somewhere. Some hand must move the
pen along or press the keys and steer, somehow, the granddaughter towards the Boston fern or place the golden apple
at the foot of the blue cradle. "A woman sat down at a table
and—"

She felt her arm fall heavy on the table and she wondered, oddly, whether or not the table objected. And was
the lamp, clamped there to the table's edge, exhausted after
so long a day? Were the floorboards reasonably cheerful or
the door numb with lack of movement, and was the broken
letter on her keyboard appeased at last by her cast-off self?

Because now her thoughts flowed through every object

and every corner of the room, and a moment later she *became* the walls and also the clean roof overhead and the powerful black sky. Why, she wondered aloud, had she stayed so long enclosed by the tough, lonely pronoun of her body when the whole world beckoned?

But the words she actually set down came from the dark eye of her eye, the stubborn self that refused at the last moment to let go. "A woman sat down—"

Everyone knew who the woman was. Even when she put a red hat on her head or changed her name or turned the clock back a thousand years or resorted to wobbly fables about granddaughters and Boston ferns, everyone knew the woman had been there from the start, seated at a table, object and subject sternly fused. No one, not even the very young, pretends that the person who brought forth words was any other than the arabesque of the unfolded self. There was no escape and scarcely any sorrow.

"A woman sat down and wrote," she wrote.

Windows

———

IN THE DAYS WHEN the Window Tax was first introduced M. J. used to say to me, "Stop complaining. Accept. Render unto Caesar. Et cetera."

I remember feeling at the time of the legislation that the two of us would continue to live moderately well as long as we had electricity to illuminate our days and nights, and failing that, kerosene or candles. But I knew that our work would suffer in the long run.

"Furthermore," M. J. continued, "the choice is ours. We can block off as many or as few windows as we choose."

This was true enough; the government, fearing rebellion, I suppose, has left the options open. Theoretically, citizens are free to choose their own level of taxation, shutting off, if they like, just one or two windows or perhaps half to two-thirds of their overall glazed area. In our own case,

we immediately decided to brick up the large pane at the
back of the house which overlooks the ravine. A picture
window is how my parents would have described this wide,
costly expanse of glass; M. J. prefers the trademark term
"panorama vista," but at the same time squints ironically
when it's mentioned. We loved the view, both of us, and felt
our work was nourished by it, those immense swaying
poplars and the sunlight breaking across the top of their
twinkling leaves, but once we sat down and calculated the
tax dollars per square inch of window, we decided we would
have to make the sacrifice.

Next we closed off our bedroom windows. Who needs
light in a bedroom, we reasoned, or the bathroom either, for
that matter? We liked to think at the time that our choices
represented a deliberate push towards optical derangement,
and that this was something that might add a certain... *je ne
sais quoi*...to a relationship that has never been easy.

Before the advent of the Window Tax, light had streamed
into our modest-but-somehow-roomy house, and both M.
J. and I rejoiced in the fact, particularly since we earn our
living as artists—I work in oils; M. J.'s medium is also oils,
but thinly, thinly applied so that the look is closer to tem-
pera. Light—natural light—was crucial to us. Just think
what natural light allows one to see: the thousand varying
shades of a late fall morning when the sky is brittle with
a blue and gold hardness, or the folded, collapsed, watery
tints of a February afternoon. Still, artificial light was better

than no light at all. We did go to the trouble of applying to the government for a professional dispensation, a matter of filling out half a dozen forms, but naturally we were turned down.

We were, it could be argued, partly prepared for our deprivation, since both of us had long since adjusted our work cycle to the seasonal rhythms, putting in longer hours in the summer and cutting back our painting time in the dark ends of winter days, quitting as early as three-thirty or four, brewing up a pot of green tea, and turning to other pursuits, occasionally pursuits of an amatory disposition; M. J.'s sensibility rises astonishingly in the midst of coziness and flickering shadow. Our most intimate moments, and our most intense, tend to fall into that crack of the day when the sun has been cut down to a bent sliver of itself and even that about to disappear on the horizon.

It is a fact that my work has always suffered at the approach of winter. The gradual threatened diminishment of the afternoon sun encourages a false exuberance. Slap down the thick blades of colour while it is still possible. Hurry. Be bold (my brain shouts and prods), and out of boldness, while the clock drains away each thrifty second of possibility, will come that accident we call art.

It seldom does. What I imagine to be a useful recklessness is only bad painting executed with insufficient light.

M. J.'s highly representational work prospers even less well than mine during the late autumn days, not that the two of us have ever spoken of this. You will understand that two painters living together under one roof can be an invitation to discord, and its lesser cousin, irritation. Ideally artists would be better off selecting mates who are civil engineers or chiropractors or those who manufacture buttons or cutlery. It's relatively easy to respect disparate work, but how do we salute, purely, the creative successes of those we live with, those we stand beside while brushing our teeth? How to rule out envy, or worse, disdain, and to resist those little sideways words or faked encouragement, delivered with the kind of candour that is really presumption? And so when I say, rather disingenuously, that M. J.'s work prospers less well, is overly representational, employs too much purple and lavender, and so on, you will have to take my pronouncement with a certain skepticism. And then reflect on the problems of artistic achievement and its measurement, and the knowledge that systems of temperament are immensely complicated. The salt and wound of M. J.'s vulnerability, for instance, is stalked by an old tenderness, but also by the fear of being overtaken.

It seems that most artists are frightened by any notion of subtraction, and, of course, the rationing of light falls into the category of serious deprivation. Without paint, artists can create images with their own blood or excrement if necessary, not that the two of us have ever been driven to such measures, but there is no real substitute for natural light. As the accustomed afternoon rays grow thinner, the work becomes more desperate, careless, and ineffectual. We often discussed this over our tea mugs during our midwinter days when the year seemed at its weakest point, how scarcity can stifle production or else, as in my case, clear a taunting space to encourage it. It seemed to both of us monumentally unfair.

But then, with the new tax measures, the house was dark all day. Like everyone else we had come to see the cutting back of natural light as a civic protest against a manipulative tax, *conscience de nos jours*, you might call it, and like all but the very rich we had filled in every one of our windows—with brick or stone or sheets of ugly plywood. *Obscura maxima* was the code phrase on our politicized tongues, and we spoke it proudly—and on our bumper stickers too—at least in the beginning. (Of course we left the window in our studio as long as we were able, and only boarded it up when we were made to feel we had failed in our civic responsibility.)

In another country, at a different latitude, we might have packed up our easels and paints and sandwiches and worked *en plein air*, since no government, however avid for revenues, is able to control access to outdoor light. But "nature's studio," as the great Linnaeus called it, is seldom available in our northern climate. Our winters are long and bitter, and our summers filled with sultry air and plagues of mosquitoes. We are dependent, therefore, on a contrived indoor space, our *atelier*, as I sometimes like to call it, into which we coax as much light as possible—or at least we did before the enactment of the Window Tax.

The tax, when it was first introduced, had a beguiling logic, and even the appearance of fairness. We know, every last one of us, how widespread the evils of tax evasion are, how even the most morally attentive—and I would put M. J. and myself in that category—inflate their travel receipts or conceal small transactions which have brought them profit. More than once I've exchanged little dashed-off paintings, still lifes mostly, for such necessities as fuel oil and roof repairs, leaving behind not a trace for my accountant's eye.

The genius of the new tax was its simplicity. Some forms of wealth can be hidden in safe-deposit boxes or in dresser drawers, but the dwellings we inhabit announce, loudly and publicly, our financial standing—their size, their aesthetic proportions, the materials with which they are fashioned. And what could be more visible from the exterior than the number and size of one's windows? What feature can be more easily calculated?

A formula was worked out: so many tax dollars per square inch of window. A populist victory.

The results might have been foreseen. Overnight, with windows an index to wealth, and thus a liability, the new form of tax evasion became, as you can imagine, a retreat to mediaeval darkness. One by one, and then hundreds by hundreds, our wondrous apertures to the world were walled in with wood or cardboard or solid masonry. As seen from the outside, the hurriedly filled-in windows gave our houses the blank, stunned look of abandonment. Inside was trapped the darkness of a primitive world; we might just as well have been living in caves or burrows.

The plotted austerities of our own domestic life, so appealing at first, soon faded. A life in the dark is close to motionless; hour by hour the outlines of our bodies are lost—there is no armature of style, no gesture, no signifying softness of the mouth. What follows is a curious amnesia of the self. I had thought that words spoken in the dark might bring back the old force of language, words becoming deeds, becoming defined moments, but I found instead that the voice in the dark puts on a dignified yet hollow sideshow, so that we ended up speaking to ourselves and not to each other.

Of course there was always the alternative of artificial light, which was in fact our only recourse. But a life performed under the burnt yellow-whiteness of electric illumination condemns us to perceptual distortion. There is that vicious snapping on and off of current, and the unvarying intensity, always predictable, yet always startling. The glare of a simple light bulb—think of it, that unhandsome utilitarian contrivance of glass and wire—insists on a sort of extracted/extruded truth, which those of us involved in long love affairs are wary of. Our postures and equivocations are harshly exposed, and the face we show the world subtly discoloured. Is there any love that doesn't in the end insist on naming itself, showing itself to other less fortunate people, oh look at me! at us!

When two people live and work under the same roof, the solitary nature of consciousness is frayed with a million threads of incalculability, and one of those threads is a decision to avoid emotional dissonance and preserve for one's self certain areas of privacy. M. J. and I, in the months following the Window Tax, settled for an unspoken equipoise: I kept my self-doubts to myself and, in turn, was spared the usual strong doses of disrespect about my *attitude*.

No longer did we discuss our work or show our projects to each other, though we occupied as always the same studio. We kept to our separate corners. I worked mainly during the day and M. J. at night, for with the loss of daylight it scarcely mattered to us anymore which was which. As for our *vie intime*, well, that had declined radically after just a few days spent under the parching electric lights. While M. J. slept, I worked steadily but with a constant ache of discouragement, attempting with my range of aromatic oils to re-create on canvas the warmth and shine of inflowing light, that which I'd known all my life but now could scarcely remember. This was a flat, dull width of time, though I have always recognized that long chapters of life go on without strong passion.

It occurred to me one day that my use of canvas might be at fault. Stretched canvas, with its stiff industrial surface,

possesses a withholding element and in the best of circumstances is reluctant at first to "open" its weave to what is
offered. I knew that it had once been customary to paint on
wood surfaces, hearty walnut planks or maple—this was
an old and honourable tradition, and one that I thought
worth trying.

At that moment my eyes fell on the slab of plywood we
had nailed over the studio window, and the thought came
to me that I might overpaint its cheap fir grain with a
diverting image: one of my tossed-off still lifes perhaps, a
collection of lemons on a blue plate or a pitcher of pure
water, something anyway that was more consoling than the
life around me and less inviting of the late afternoon fits
and starts brought on by the overhead lights.

The rectangularity of the wood seemed to demand a
frame of some kind, and this I carefully painted in, exchanging the rather harsh oranginess of fir for a subtly
grained and bevelled oak, a generous four inches in width,
working my way around the two sides, the top and bottom,
and then, finally, painting in a quartet of fine mitred corners. An easy trick, you might think, transforming one type
of wood into another, but the task took me the rest of the
day—and half of the next.

When I paint I am composed, I am most truly myself,
but I wish I could tell you how much happiness this particular craftsmanlike task gave me, exchanging wood for simple wood, coaxing ripples from dead surfaces. My usual

paintings are compositionally complex and employ a rich colour field. I am known for my use of the curved line. It's even been said that my management of the curve has brought to contemporary painting "an engagement for the eye and a seduction for the intellect." And yet, the strict linearity of my new "oak" frame brought a satisfaction my rondure illusions have never given.

At first I didn't know that what I was framing was, in fact, a window; the knowledge came upon me slowly as I found my brush dividing the framed space into a series of smaller rectangles, bringing about a look that was oddly architectural. Again I reached for a golden oakiness of colour; again I kept my lines disciplined and sharp, but narrower now, more delicate and refined.

Mullions. The word leapt into my head. A relic of an older world from a wiser consciousness. These nonstructural bars dividing the lights or panes of the window proved relatively easy to master, being simple wood strips, slightly grooved on their edges, glinting with their barely revealed woody highlights. Each one of them pleased me, the verticals, the horizontals, and most especially their shy intersections.

That phrase *most especially.* Did you notice? M. J. has no patience with such locutions.

Harder to paint on the surface of ordinary plywood was the image of glass, and so I was forced to experiment. Window glass, as you will have observed, is a curious half-silvered substance, a steaming liquid that has been frozen into a solid plane. Glass possesses different colours at different hours of the day. Sometimes it pretends it's a mirror. Other times it gathers checks and streaks and bubbles of brilliance and elegant flexes of mood. Its transparency winks back at you, yet it withholds, in certain weathers, what is on the other side, revealing only a flash of wet garden grass, a shadow of a close-standing hedge, or perhaps a human figure moving across its width—the mail carrier or a neighbour or even M. J. out for a late afternoon stroll. Glass is green like water or blue like the sky or a rectangle of beaten gold when the setting sun strikes it or else a midnight black broken by starlight or the cold courteous reflection of the moon.

Glassiness evaded me. My brush halted; it swung in the air like a metronome. What I produced were grey cloudy squares with a cardboardlike density, a kindergarten version of what a window might be.

It may have been that I was tired. Or that I was visited by that old fear of failure or by the sense of lowered consequence that arrives out of nowhere, especially when I hear M. J. tiptoeing around in the kitchen, brewing yet another pot of tea. I decided to leave it until morning.

As always I rose early and went straight to the studio and snapped on the electric lights. My "window" was waiting, but I saw immediately that it was altered. The shadows of my oak mouldings had acquired a startling trompe l'oeil vividness, their depth and shadow augmented and their woodiness enlivened by amber flecks and streaks. I had been pleased to arrive the day before at a primitive suggestiveness —window as architectural detail, window as gesturing towards windowness, just falling short of veri-similitude, but this was now a window so cunningly made that it could almost have been opened on its casement hinges. Hinges that had not existed yesterday. The glass panes too had been tampered with. I looked closely and recognized a slick oil shine superimposed on a lake of rainy mauve.

All day I worked on the glass. It went slowly, so slowly that often an hour would pass with only one or two touches of my brush on the surface. My paint was mixed and layered, rubbed out, then reapplied. By evening I had managed to articulate, or so I thought, the spark and glance and surprise of glass without, of course, stretching towards the achievement of light or air.

I woke the next morning with a sense of excitement. Even before entering the studio I could feel a soft-shoe dance in the region of my chest, and I reflected that it had been some years since my feelings had run so dangerously out of control. My "window" shone, its oak frame burning with an almost antique burnish, and the troublesome panes giving off their glassy gifts. How is it possible to make light dance on a flat surface, and how does anyone bring transparency to what is rigid and unyielding? I sighed, then readied myself for a day of work.

It was at least a week before the task was done. By coincidence we were both there when it reached completion, standing side by side in one of our rare moments of tenderness, each of us with brush in hand. One of us reached forward to apply a final brush-stroke, though we weren't able to remember afterwards which it was. The moment was beautiful, but also blurred. We recall a sudden augmentation of brilliance, as though we witnessed the phenomenon with a single pair of eyes, our "window" bursting its substance, freed in such a way that light flowed directly through it.

Not real light, of course, but the idea of light—infinitely more alluring than light itself. Illusion, accident, meticulous attention all played a part in the construction of a window that had become more than a window, better than a window, the window that would rest in the folds of the mind as all that was ideal and desirable in the opening, beckoning, sensuous world.

Reportage

———

N OW THAT A ROMAN arena has been discovered in southeastern Manitoba, the economy of this micro-region has been transformed. Those legendary wheat farms with their proud old family titles have gone wilfully, happily bankrupt, gone "bust" as they say in the area, and the same blond, flat-lying fields that once yielded forty bushels per acre have been turned over to tourism.

Typical is the old Orchard place off Highway 12. Last Wednesday I visited Mr. Orchard in the sunny ranch-style house he shares with his two cocker bitches, Beauty and Trude, one of them half blind, the other hard of hearing. The fir floors of the Orchard place shine with lemon wax. There are flowers in pottery vases and the walls are covered by the collage works of his former wife, Mavis, who is said to be partly responsible for the discovery and excavation of the Roman ruins. I asked Mr. Orchard for a brief history.

"Quite early on," he mused, pouring out cups of strong Indian tea, "I became aware of a large shallow depression in the west quarter of our family farm. The depression, circular in shape like a saucer and some ninety metres across, was not so much visible to the eye as experienced by the body. Whenever I rode tractor in this area—I am speaking now of my boyhood—I anticipated, and registered, this very slight dip in the earth's surface, and then the gradual rise and recovery of level ground. We referred to this geological anomaly as Billy's Basin for reasons which I cannot now recall, although I did have an Uncle Bill on my mother's side who farmed in the area in the years before the Great War, a beard-and-twinkle sort of fellow and something of a scholar according to family legend, who was fond of sitting up late and reading by lamplight—books, newspapers, mail-order catalogues, anything the man could get his hands on. I have no doubt but that he was familiar with the great Greek and Roman civilizations, but certainly he never dreamed that the remnants of antiquity were so widely spread as to lie buried beneath our own fertile fields here in Manitoba and that his great-grandnephew—myself, that is—would one day derive his living not from wheat but from guiding tours and selling postcards. Whether Uncle Bill would have scorned or blessed this turn of events I have no way of knowing, but I like to think he was not a man to turn his back on fortune."

At that point one of Mr. Orchard's dogs, Beauty, rubbed voluptuously against his trousers leg. "You will agree with me," he said, "that once a thing is discovered, there's no way on earth to undiscover it."

Mavis Orchard (née Gulching), who has been amicably separated from Mr. Orchard for the last six months, was able to fill me in on the circumstances of the actual discovery. She is an attractive, neatly dressed woman of about sixty with thick, somewhat wayward iron-grey hair and a pleasant soft-spoken manner. Smilingly, she welcomed me to her spacious mobile home outside Sandy Banks and, despite the hour, insisted on making fresh coffee and offering a plateful of homemade cinnamon-spiral rolls. Her collage work was everywhere in evidence, and centred more and more, she told me, on the metaphysics of time, Kiros and Chronos, and the disjunctive nature of space/matter. She is a woman with a decidedly philosophic turn of mind, but whose speech is braced by an unflinching attachment to the quotidian.

"When we think of the fruits of the earth," she led off, "we tend to think of cash crops or mineral deposits. We think"—and she held up her meticulously manicured hands and ticked off a list—"of wheat. Of oil. Of phosphates. Natural gas. Even gold. Gold does occur. But the last thing we think of finding is a major historical monument of classical proportions."

At this she shrugged hyperbolically in a way that indicated her sense of the marvellous. "Arrowheads, of course, have been found in this area from early times. Also a small but unique wooden sundial displayed now in the Morden Local History Museum, where you can also see a fine old English axe belonging to the first settler in this region, a Mr. DeBroches. But"—and she tugged at her off-white woollen cardigan, resettling it around her rather amply formed shoulders—"when the drills went into our west quarter section looking for oil and came up hard against three supine Ionic columns, we knew we were on to something of import and significance, and that there could be no turning back. This earth of ours rolls and rolls through its mysterious vapours. Who would want to stop it? Not I."

Angela and Herbert Penner, whose back porch offers the best position from which to photograph the ruined arena, spoke openly to me about the changes that have overtaken their lives.

Herbert: There are problems, of course, adjusting to a new economic base.

Angela: I wish they wouldn't throw things on the ground, gum wrappers, plastic wrap from their sandwiches, and so on. Last summer our family cat Frankie swallowed a soft drink tab and had to be taken to the vet, which set us back fifty dollars if you can believe it. But most people who come here are just people.

Herbert: (proudly) We've had visitors from all fifty states,
              all ten Canadian provinces plus the territories,
              Western Europe, Japan, and mainland China.

Angela: Would you like to see the guest book? One gen-
              tleman wrote recently: "Standing at the entrance
              to this site, one experiences a sort of humility."

Herbert: (piqued) A lady from California wrote: "Not
              nearly as impressive as Nîmes."

Angela: That's in France. Theirs seats twenty thousand.

Herbert: Not the point really, though, is it?

Angela: We've managed to keep our charges reasonable.
              Our colour film we sell at almost cost.

Herbert: (interrupting) Coffee and sandwiches is where
              we make our bit of change, I'd say. Refresh-
              ments. Think about that word. Re-fresh-ments.

Angela: And next year we're edging into B and B.

Herbert: Meaning bed and breakfast.

Angela: All in all we feel we've been blessed.

Herbert: (concludingly) Oh, richly, richly blessed.

   Dr. Elizabeth Jane Harkness at the Interpretative
Centre replied somewhat caustically when asked about the
markings on the stones and columns, "The motifs we find
here are perhaps closer to the cup-and-ring carvings of
prehistory than to the elaborate texts found on most
traditional Roman structures," she admitted, patting her
handsome auburn hair in place, "but we find it offensive
and indeed Eurocentric to have *our* markings referred to

as 'doodles.' It is one of the great romances of consciousness to think that language is the only form of containment and continuity, but who nowadays really subscribes? Who? Our simple markings here, which I personally find charming and even poignant, are as emblematically powerful in their way as anything the Old World has to offer."

Jay DeBroches, former grain-elevator manager and great-grandson of the first settler in the area, took me along to the Sandy Banks beer hall, now renamed the Forum, and said very quietly, with innate dignity, "Speaking off record for a moment, there was a certain amount of skepticism at first, and although I don't like to say so, most of it came from south of the border. It was like we-had-a-Roman-ruin-and-they-didn't sort of thing. One guy claimed it was an elaborate hoax. A Disneyesque snow job. Like we'd done it with mirrors. Well, they sent their big boys up here for a look-see, and one glance at this gorgeous multitiered, almost perfect circle was enough to convince them of what was what. Now we've got some kind of international trustee setup, and that keeps them happy, though rumour has it they're scouring Minnesota and North Dakota with laser-graphs looking for one of their own, but so far no luck. I guess in my heart of hearts I hope ours is the only one. I've got the parking concession, so I'm here every morning early, and it still makes me shiver—even my fingers shiver, every little joint—when I see the dew winking off these immense old shelfy stones and giving a sense of the monolithic enterprise of that race that came before us."

The Stanners family has thus far concentrated on T-shirts, felt pennants, and key-rings, what Mrs. Stanners refers to as "your takeaway trade." But she has visions of outdoor concerts, even opera. "And this place is a natural for Disney-on-Ice," she says, escorting me to her veranda and offering a wicker armchair.

San (Salvador) Petty, chief zoning officer, unrolls a set of maps and flattens them on a table. I help him weigh down the edges with desktop oddments, a stapler, an onyx pen holder, a framed photograph of the arena itself during the early stages of excavation. "Here," Mr. Petty explains, pointing with the eraser end of a pencil, "is where the new highway will come. The north and south arms join here, and as you can see we've made allowance for state-of-the-art picnic facilities. We have a budget for landscaping, we have a budget for future planning and contingency costs and the development of human resources. None of this just happened, we made it happen."

"Speaking personally," said retired Latin teacher Ruby Webbers, "I believe it is our youth who will ultimately suffer. The planting and harvesting of grain were honourable activities in our community and gave our boys and girls a sense of buoyancy and direction. They felt bonded to the land, not indebted to it. I don't know, I just don't know. Sometimes I walk over here to the site on moist, airy evenings, just taking in the spectacle of these ancient quarried stones, how their edges sharpen under the floodlights and how they spread themselves out in wider and wider circles. Suddenly my throat feels full of bees. I want to cry. Why not? Why are you looking at me like that? I grant you it's beautiful, but do beautiful monuments ever think of the lives they smash? Oh, I feel my whole body start to tremble. It shouldn't be here. It has nothing to do with us. It scares me. You're not listening to me, are you? At times it seems to be getting even bigger and more solid and more *there*. It preens, it leers. If I could snap my fingers and make it disappear, that's what I'd do. Just snap, snap, and say, 'Vanish, you ridiculous old phantom—shoo!'"

Edith-Esther

—

EDITH-ESTHER'S BIOGRAPHER started phoning her a year ago wanting to know her thoughts about God.

Generally he manages to catch her early in the morning, just as she's rubbing her creased eyes open and setting aside her night dreams, reaching sideways for her bathrobe, coughing her habitual morning cough.

She's noticed how he can be aggressive in his questioning or else placatory, depending on how the biography is going or what he judges her mood to be. "It's most interesting," he said one day, purring into the mouthpiece, "that you seem not to have addressed or referenced a single particularized deity in any of your novels."

"Really?" she said, belting her robe against the morning chill. "Can that be true?"

"Not unless you count the paragraph in *Lest We Be*

Known, Chapter Four, page twelve of the first edition, when George Hellman says something or other about how God has damned the entire Hellman dynasty."

"Oh, hmmmm, yes." She is holding the phone tucked under her chin, which is more painful than one might think, while she struggles to find the on switch for her new Swiss coffee machine. "I think I did say something like that."

"But my sense, Edith-Esther, is that you intend this particular aside to be more metaphorical than specific."

"I believe you must be right," she said. She is eighty years old, and more and more finds that the novels she's written, their textures, their buzzing, inhabited worlds, blend into the width of a long grassy field. Or rather, the various novels can be reduced to a single brevity. Love doubted. Love lost, love renounced. Bleak, she often thinks to herself of her own work. Or, when she wants to treat herself kindly, austere.

"It would be useful," her biographer said, "if you could state, one way or another, on which side of the belief debate you sit."

"Debate?"

There! She'd found the switch. In a few minutes there would be four inches of coffee in the glass pot, dark and flavourful, a Brazilian blend, her daily ration. With coffee she would be set for the morning, held alert and upright. "Now, which debate would you be referring to?"

They both recognized that she was being disingenuous. Stalling.

"The classic debate, Edith-Esther. Does He or does He not exist?"

"I'm surprised at you," she said. "You of all people even raising the question, and in that form."

"What can I say? A biographer is obliged to raise all questions. The total weave of personality must include—"

"I don't believe," she told him plainly, "in God."

Did she imagine him sighing? Yes. There was a silence, at any rate, just spacious enough to enclose a sigh. "What's wanted, Edith-Esther, is some slight spiritual breeze blowing through the life material, the merest hint of the unseen world."

This was too much for Edith-Esther, who had spent her life in flight from those who believe the body merely a sack for the soul. "I would have thought," she said, "that a man like you might appreciate that we live in secular times, and that the next century will be even more—"

"I wasn't speaking of a whole theological system. Good heavens, no. Your readers would never"—here he produced one of his small, appeasing, updraught chuckles—"expect any such thing. I think they'd be happy with just, you know, some small tossed coin at the fountain of faith. Some offhand salute to a Creator or Supreme Being. Or even the mention of an occasion when you reflected, however briefly, on the nature of the Life Force."

Life Force? The term, so old-fashioned and Shavian, brought her a smile. She looked down, and abruptly stopped smiling. Her left arm displayed a veiny ridge of fine purple. Was it there yesterday?

She poured a stream of coffee into a thin white mug and sipped cautiously, seeing even without the aid of a mirror how her upper lip puckered grotesquely at the ceramic edge, trembling and sucking like a baby's greedy mouth. She was at an age when eating and drinking should be done in private. "I may have reflected on such matters," she said, "but I was not at any time rewarded with proof."

"I see." Disappointment raised his voice to a croak. "Well, perhaps I might say that in the biography, quote those very words you've just uttered."

"No, absolutely not. That would give a false impression. That I'm some sort of desperately seeking pilgrim."

Edith-Esther can imagine her biographer at this moment, a hundred and twelve green miles away, past four loops of major highway, across a concrete bridge, eighteen storeys into the air, sitting at his blocky desk and holding a Bic straight up on its point, trying to think of another angle from which he might approach the subject of Edith-Esther's non-existent religious impulse.

She understood how careful you had to be with biographers; death by biography—it was a registered disease. Thousands have suffered from it, butchery by entrapment in the isolated moment. The selected moment with its carbon lining. Biographers were forever catching you out and reminding you of what you once said. *But back in 1974 you stated categorically that...*

He was, if only he knew, just one centimetre more tactful and patient than she actually demanded. It was exasperating, but also amusing, the way he tiptoed, advanced, and withdrew, then advanced again. She supposed this show of courtesy masked his very real powers of extraction and was what made him who he was—one of the world's most successful and respected biographers, at least in the literary arena. Robert Sillerman, Roche Clement, Amanda Bishop—he'd done them all. His portrait of the prickly Wilfred Holmsley was considered a model of a private life turned inside out, yet each of its revelations seemed perfectly stitched in place so that nothing really surprised or shocked, not even the disclosure of Holmsley's plagiarism in his late sixties, that dramatic accident scene, lifted almost word for word from a newspaper report. (Inadvertent, the judge ruled when the case came to trial, a question of Mr. Holmsley copying an arresting text into his notebook and forgetting the quote marks. Also pertinent was the question of just how many ways it was possible to describe a simple decapitation.)

"Well, then," Edith-Esther's biographer continued, "do you believe in anything at all?"

She considered. "I suppose you must mean astrology or tea leaves or something of that sort."

"I mean," he said, "just anything. *Anything.*"

"For some reason I have the sense you're trying to bully me into belief, and I'm not sure that's fair. Or useful."

"Not at all, Edith-Esther, not at all. No biographer worth his or her professional salt manipulates the material. Or the subject. Don't even entertain the thought. Pulling cords of memory is what I'm really trying to do. Helping you to put a finger on some moment, partly obscured perhaps, that would be perfectly understandable, when you might have, you know, transcended this world for an instant and then buried it in the text, which is something writers are wont to do, and—"

"Do you remember when you and I signed our initial agreement two years ago this March?"

"Of course. A wonderful occasion."

"Which we celebrated, you'll recall, with dinner at Mr. Chan's."

"The most delicate shrimp dumplings I've ever had the pleasure of tasting. Little clouds, saffron-scented. We actually asked the waiter to refill the serving dish, didn't we?"

"And do you remember the moment when the fortune cookies arrived?"

"How could I forget? Oh! Oh! Mine said, 'Persevere and you will arrive at truth.'"

"You will also recollect that I refused to open my fortune cookie."

"Because—"

"I knew I was disappointing you, but I am less willing than some to be drawn into the realm of the spurious and superstitious. You will remember that I was not what is known as a good sport that evening."

"Come, now, Edith-Esther, no one really believes in fortune cookies."

"You did, at least on that particular occasion. You decreed it was an omen. By perseverance you are going to arrive at the truth of my life. I believe you called it my 'kernel of authenticity.'"

"Oh, yes. That!"

"I admit I was troubled by the phrase. Thinking to myself, what if there were no kernel, what then?"

"I never meant to put forward something you'd find disturbing—"

"I must have lost my rationality, at least for a moment. The fact is, I slipped my fortune cookie into my handbag and brought it home. Just before going to bed I opened it up."

"Bless you, dear Edith-Esther. And what did it say?"

"It informed me that romance was about to enter my life."

"Ah."

"Now do you see why I reject all projections from beyond?"

"But your opening of the fortune cookie suggests, in a sense, your willingness to test your faith."

"Absolutely not," she said, draining her cup. "It suggests the opposite. A test of my disbelief."

One day Edith-Esther's biographer phoned earlier than usual. He was excited. He'd found something. "I've been rereading *Wherefore Bound*," he said.

Wherefore Bound. She tried to remember which one that was. Part of an early trilogy. The second volume? Or else the first. The air in front of her eyes filled for a moment with a meadow landscape, classic birds, wild grasses, a blur of shredded cloud. "Oh, yes," she said.

"Remember Paul Sinclair? He's the defrocked priest, the one who renounces his faith and—"

"Of course I remember."

"Your strongest work, in the opinion of the more astute critics—that tiny, ever-diminishing troupe. What I mean is, the character of Paul Sinclair is densely and beguilingly ambiguous."

"I wouldn't say ambiguous, not at all, in fact." She raised her cup to her mouth. Her coffee machine was broken. It was under guarantee, but so far she has been unable to find the required certificate. Meanwhile, she was making do with Nescafé, which she found bitter. "I'd say Paul Sinclair is very firm in his position."

"The fact is, Edith-Esther, he repeats and repeats his disconnection with the Godhead."

"Wouldn't you say that shows—"

"He repeats himself so often that one begins to doubt his doubt. Don't you see? Protesting too much? It seems very clear to me. Faith's absence pressed to the wall and brought to question. And then he leads the hundred children on their march and later overcomes—"

"He never admits anything."

"I was caught too by the symbolism of his lover's name. Magdelena. Now, there's a name with spiritual resonance, oh, my, yes, and—"

"I've always liked that name. I met someone a long time ago in Mexico named Magdelena, who became—"

"And there's the place where you're talking about Magdelena's lips and you say—surely you remember—you say, 'her lips form a wound in her flesh.'"

"I can't believe I said anything as silly as that."

"Wounds, Edith-Esther. The wounds of Christ? Surely that rings a ding-dong."

"I must have been trying to describe the *colour* of her lips, their redness, something like that. Perhaps they were chapped. Perhaps she was suffering from cold sores. I myself used to be troubled by—"

"You've always undervalued your own work, Edith-Esther. Rejected any sense of subtext, even when it's staring you in the face."

"I've never—"

"Why is it you're always refusing comfort? Why?"

"I don't know." She really didn't. Though perhaps she

couldn't help thinking, it was because she'd refused to offer her readers the least crumb of comfort.

"Never mind, forgive me. It's part of your charm, Edith-Esther. It's all right. It's you."

"My kernel of authenticity?"

"What a memory you have. You're teasing me, I know, feeding me back my own nonsense. *Une taquine.* Even over the telephone wire, I can hear you teasing. But yes, it's true. You're exactly who you are."

"Whoever that may be."

"Hello?"

"Good morning, Edith-Esther. It's me."

"So early."

"I've been up all night rereading *Sacred Alliance*."

"Well"—she gave a laugh, rather a wobbly one—"I'm afraid you can't describe *that* one as a critical success."

"Because it was misunderstood. I mean that with all my heart. I misunderstood it myself, initially. That word *Sacred* in the title, it completely escaped me until last night, but now I see exactly the flag you were waving."

"Flag? Waving? Oh, my. The title, I'm quite sure, was meant to be ironic. I'm certain that was my intention. It's so long ago, though, and I just this minute woke up. I can't seem to find my glasses. I know they're here somewhere. Perhaps I should phone you back when I'm feeling more focused—"

"You remember when Gloria first meets Robin, page fifty-one, and admits the fact of her virginity to him, it all comes out in a burst, not surprisingly, but what she's really saying is that she's made a choice, a sacred choice, a declaration about where she ultimately intends to place her devotion—"

"I can't imagine what I did with those glasses. I left them on the bedside table last night—"

"—and so, when Gloria and Robin go off to Vienna together and after that most unsatisfactory consummation et cetera, and when he goes out to arrange for a rental car and she locks herself in the hotel room—remember?—and writes him a note—"

"They're broken. One of the lenses. The left one. Smashed. I simply can't understand it—"

"—and the key word in that note is in the last line, the word *intact*. She writes that she wants to keep their one glorious night together *intact*, but what she's really saying is—"

"Oh, God!"

"Edith-Esther?"

She seemed to be stumbling across a width of unlevelled ground, still wet with the morning's dew. "I'll have to phone you back, I can't seem to—"

"—that she will choose celibacy, that her calling lies in the realm of the spiritual, and that she—Are you there, Edith-Esther? Hello? Hello?"

———

"Just a quick call. Hope I didn't wake you."

"I was just lying here dozing. Feeling guilty. Thinking about getting up."

"I had to know. Have you seen the book?"

"Which book?"

"*The* book. Your biography. *A Spiritual Odyssey?*"

"Oh."

"Surely it arrived. Surely you've had a chance to look at it."

"I've been a little under the weather. Just twinges. And my glasses are broken again."

"You're not seriously ill, surely."

"Too many birthdays. As they say."

"Not you, Edith-Esther. Not someone with your spirit."

"My spirit? My what?"

"The cover. What do you think of the cover?"

"Very arresting. It turned out well. But the title—when did you decide to change the title?"

"Last-minute kind of thing. The publisher and I agreed it captured the direction your life has taken."

"You took out that part in the second chapter about my first communion."

"No, it's there. I just gave it a slightly different inter-pretation."

"I dropped the host on the church floor and stepped on it."

"You may remember it that way, but in fact—"

"It's just ordinary bread, I remember saying to myself. Store bread. White bread. I wanted to see if there'd be any lightning bolts."

"You were very young. And probably excited. You dropped it by accident, and were so embarrassed you tried to cover it—the host, that is—with your foot."

"There were no lightning bolts. I was sure there wouldn't be. There was nothing, only a hard, accusing look from the priest."

"He understood your embarrassment."

"His name was Father Albert. You left out his name."

"He could still be living."

"He'd have to be a hundred and ten."

"There might be a lawsuit, though. From the Church."

"Because he liked little girls? Liked to tickle them under the arms and between the legs?"

"The implications, that's all."

"You should have asked me—"

"It isn't what people want to hear, Edith-Esther. They've heard too much of that particular story in recent years. You'd be charged with a psychological cliché, I'm afraid."

"Clichés are almost always true—have you noticed that?"

"I don't want to see you represented as one of those insipid victims—"

"I saw early on that my particular kind was considered dangerous and needed to be locked up—in the house, in the convent. Did you know women were excluded from the Latin discourse?"

"Other times, other rhymes."

"I haven't been well."

"You sound extremely weak, Edith-Esther. Your voice. Have you seen a doctor?"

"Do you think I should?"

"I can't possibly know. But I can tell you one thing. The book is getting a positive response."

"Really?"

"More than positive. The fact is, people are finding it uplifting."

"Up-what?"

"I know you detest the word. And the concept. But some of us haven't your strength. We need encouragement along the way."

"I never meant to be uplifting. The last thing I wanted was to—"

"Of course not. But your example, Edith-Esther. All you've been through. The way you've translated your spiritual struggle into enlightenment."

"My glasses are broken."

"I'm praying that it hits the best-seller lists by next week."

"You're praying? Is that what you said?"

"Edith-Esther, are you there?"

No, she is no longer there. She's walking down the long green hummocky field, which may not be a field at all but a garden in a state of ruin. Whatever it is, it slopes towards a mere trickle of a river, and this is disappointing, the reluctant flow of water over small white stones, and also the surprising unevenness of the terrain. Ugly, ugly, seen up close. She feels, or else hears, one of her ankles snap. Chitinous. Oh, God. Barbed weeds and rough sedges, they scratch her bare legs and thighs. Luckily she has the sense to squeeze her eyes shut and to make tight fists of her hands. Every muscle in her body tenses against a possible invasion of bees or whatever else might come.

Some years ago Edith-Esther's pencil jar was stolen from her kitchen by an avid literary groupie. An image of this plain glass jar returns to her at the very moment she stumbles and falls. Probably, before its pencil-jar incarnation, it had held her favourite redcurrant jelly. Its glassy neck was comfortably wide, the more freely to receive her sharpened pencils and a fat pink eraser with old rubbed edges. There was a serious pair of scissors too, black-handled, and what else? She was forgetting something. Oh, yes. A decorative letter opener given to her by a friend—Magdelena?—with the Latin words RARA AVIS stamped on the handle. A rare bird.

She feels herself grasping the handle now and testing the blade against her arm. It is surprisingly sharp, so sharp she decides to hack at the savage purple grass rising up around her, clearing a path for herself, making her way forward.

New Music

———

S HE WAS TWENTY-ONE when he first saw her, seated
rather primly next to him on the Piccadilly Line, head-
ing towards South Kensington. It was midafternoon. Like
every other young woman in London, she was dressed from
head to toe in a shadowless black, and on her lap sat a
leather satchel.

It was the sort of satchel a girl might inherit from
her adoring barrister father, and this was the truth of
the matter (he found out later), except that the father was
a piano teacher, not a barrister, and that his adoration
was often shaded by exasperation—which one can understand.

After a moment of staring straight ahead, she snapped
open her satchel, withdrawing several sheets of paper cov-

ered with musical notations. (*He* was on his way to Imperial
College for a lecture on reinforced concrete; *she* was about
to attend an advanced class in Baroque music.) He had
never before seen anyone "read" music in quite this way,
silently, as though it were a newspaper, her eyes running
back and forth, left to right, top of the page to the bottom, then flipping to the next. The notes looked cramped
and fussy and insistent, but she took in every one, blinking
only when she shifted to a new page. He imagined that
her head was filled with a swirl of musical lint, that she
was actually "hearing" a tiny concert inside that casually
combed head of hers. And *his* head?—it was crammed with
different stuff: equations, observations, a set of graphs, the
various gradients of sands and gravels, his upcoming exam-
inations, and the fact that his trousers pocket had a hole
in it, leaking a shower of coins on to the floor as he
stood up.

"I think this is yours," she said, handing him a dropped
penny.

"Whose music is that?" he managed. "The music you're
looking at?"

"Tallis. Thomas Tallis."

"Oh."

She took pity on him as they stepped together onto the
platform. "Sixteenth-century. English."

"Is he?"—inane question—"is he good?"

"Good?"

"His music?—is it, you know, wonderful? Is he a genius, would you say?"

She stopped and considered. They were in the street now. The sunshine was sharply aslant. "He was the most gifted composer of his time," she recited, "until the advent of William Byrd."

"You mean this Byrd person came along and he was better than Thomas What's-his-name?"

"Oh"—she looked affronted—"I don't think better is quite the word. William Byrd was more inventive than Thomas Tallis, that's all. More original, in my opinion anyway."

"Then why"—this seemed something he had to know, even though his reasoning was sure to strike her as simplistic and stupid—"why are you carrying around Thomas Tallis's music instead of the other chap's—the one who was better?"

She stared at him. Then she smiled and shrugged. "Do you always insist on the very best?"

"I don't know," he said, not being someone who'd experienced much in the way of choices. He was conscious of his hideous ignorance and inability to express himself. "It just seems like a waste of time. You know, taking second best when you could have the best."

"Like reading, hmmm, Marlowe when you could have Shakespeare?"

He nodded, or at least attempted to nod.

"It's *because* I believe Tallis is second best that I prefer him," she told him then. Her chin went up. Her voice was firm. "I don't expect you to understand."

"I do, I do," he exclaimed in his awful voice. And it was true, he did.

He loved her. Right from that instant, the way she opened up her mouth and said *because Tallis is second best.*

Imagine a woman getting out of bed one hour earlier than the rest of the household. What will she do with that hour?

Make breakfast scones for her husband and three school-age children? Not this woman, not scones, banish the thought. Will she press her suit skirt? clean out her handbag? ready her attaché case for a day at work? No, this woman works at home—at a computer set up in what was once, in another era, in another incarnation, a sewing room. It's a room with discoloured wallpaper, irises climbing on a sort of trellis, which doesn't make sense for a non-climbing, earthbound flower. Against one wall is her writing table, which is really a cheap plywood door laid flat on trestles. She has been offered several times, a proper desk, but she actually prefers this makeshift affair—which wobbles slightly each time she puts her elbow on the table and stares into the screen.

That's where she is now. At this hour! Her old and not-very-clean mauve dressing gown is pulled tight against the chill. It is not a particularly flattering colour, but she doesn't know this, and besides, she's as faithful to old clothes as she is to inferior wallpaper. It's as though she can't bear to hurt their feelings. She's tapping away, without so much as a cup of coffee to cheer her on. It's still dark outside, not black exactly but a brew of streaked grey. You'd think she'd put up a curtain or at least a blind to soften that staring grey rectangle, but no. Nor has she thought to turn on the radio for a little musical companionship, she of all people. She's tapping, tapping at her keyboard, her two index fingers taking turns, and for the moment that's all she appears to need.

Is she writing a letter to her mother in Yorkshire? A Letter to the Editor complaining about access ramps for the handicapped? A suicide note full of blame and forgiveness and deliberate little shafts of self-pity? No. Today she's writing the concluding page (page 612) of a book, a book she's been working on for four years now, the comprehensive biography of Renaissance composer Thomas Tallis, ca. 1505–1585. The penultimate paragraph is already on the screen, then the concluding paragraph itself, and now, as a scarf of soft light flows in through the window and lands on her shoulders, she taps in the last sentence, and then the final word—which is the burnished, heightened, blurted-out word "triumph." The full sentence reads: "Nevertheless Tallis's contribution to English music can be described as a triumph."

Nevertheless? What's all this *nevertheless* about, you're probably asking?

Squinting into the screen, she taps in "The End," but immediately deletes it. My guess is that she's decided writing "The End" is too self-conscious a gesture. Did her husband write "The End" when he finished his monograph *Distribution of Gravel Resources in Southwest England*? Yes, certainly, but then he's not as fearful of self-indulgence as she.

She's spent four years on this book. I've already said that, haven't I?—but to be fair, the first eight months were passed listening to Tallis's music itself. The Mass for Four Voices, *Spem in alium, Lamentations of Jeremiah*, nine motets, and so on. She lay on our canted, worn sofa—the kids at school, the husband at the office—and listened with note pad and pencil on her sweatered chest, waiting for the magnetic atoms of musical matter to come together, one and one and one, and give shape to the man who created them. There's so little known about him, and what is known is made blurry with *might have, could have, possibly was*—all the maddening italics of a rigorously undocumented life. The only real resource is the music, which, curiously, has come down to our century intact, or so I'm told, and that is why this woman spent eight months absorbing each separate, self-contained, cellular note.

Occasionally she fell asleep during those long sofa days. I'm no expert, but I've been told that Tallis is not particularly interested in counterpoint as such, and that the straightforward way he develops his musical ideas produces a sense of serenity which can be an invitation to doze. She admits this, but insists he can be experimental when he wants to be and even mildly extravagant. (*In nomine* she gives as an example.)

Tallis's ghost lives in our house, his flat, hummy, holy tones and the rise and fall of Latin phrasing; it's permeated the carpets and plaster; it clings to the family hair and clothing and gets into the food. And for several months now an inky photocopy of his portrait has been stuck on the fridge, a little wraith of a man with a small pointed beard and abundant shoulder-length hair brushed back from his forehead. He is vain about his hair, one can tell.

It's not easy to calculate overall height from a head-and-shoulder image, but clearly he's got the alarmed, doubting eyes of a short man. (I am not a particularly tall chap myself, and so I instantly recognize and connect with a short man's uneasy gaze.) The children are forever asking their mother how Tom Tallis is getting along, meaning is she going to finish her book soon. They miss her rhubarb crumble, they miss the feel of ironed clothes and clean sheets and socks sorted into pairs. Her husband—he's in the sand and gravel business—he misses waking up beside her in the morning. By the time the alarm goes at half-past seven, the bed is cold, and she's already been working for an hour or more at her secondhand word processor.

"There's cornflakes," she calls out when she hears footsteps in the kitchen, not for a moment lifting her eyes from the screen. "There's plenty of bread for toast." Well, sometimes there is and sometimes there isn't.

But because this is the final morning in the writing of her book, with the book's closing word "triumph" winking at her from the screen, she rises and stretches and makes her way to the kitchen, a sleepy, mauve-toned phantom. There she finds them—two sons, daughter, and spouse, gathered about the toaster. She stares as though we are strangers who have entered her house sometime during the last four years and are now engaged in a mystical rite around this small smudged appliance. We're not exactly unwelcome, her look tells us, but the nature of our presence has yet to be explained.

Two months later Thomas Tallis is still on the fridge door. No one in the family has quite the courage to take him down, but the manuscript, all 612 pages, has been mailed to the publisher. This is a reasonably distinguished publishing house—though certainly not the best—and the editor is delighted to have the Tallis book on his fall list. He would much rather the author had written about William Byrd, of course, that goes without saying. There would have been *great* interest in a book about William Byrd, whereas there is only *considerable* interest in Thomas Tallis. Tallis, if the truth be known, must always be identified along with his famous student who, according to tradition, overshadowed him. Part of Tallis's essence, in fact, is that he is stuck in an inevitable frame of reference. He also ran. Ran a good race, but...

Imagine what a woman does who has suddenly, after four long years, completed an arduous task. She cleans her house, for one thing, not perfectly, but competently. She remains in bed an hour longer in the morning, and for this her husband is ecstatically grateful. They wake together, his lips trace the pearled curve of her spinal column. He is a man who stumbles about all day dealing with the exigencies of gravel production, gravel deliveries, gravel prices per cubic metre, but thinking every other minute of his wife's soft limbs, her bodily clefts and swellings.

For her clever daughter she buys tickets to the ballet, and they return from the performance drunk with pleasure, and enact mock, foolish pirouettes on the hall carpet, bumping into the walls and giggling like a pair of teenagers.

For her younger son, a boy of exceptional beauty, she spends a whole day sorting through the debris of his bedroom. She does this tactfully, tidily, thoroughly, and the child is conscious of an immense sense of relief. All those buried socks, books, pencil ends, wads of paper, coins, dust—he was unable to deal with it, but now all is order and ease.

Her middle child is neither clever nor exceptional in appearance, but she loves him best; she can't help it; he touches a spot of tenderness in her that only music has been able to reach. She kisses the top of his head while he eats his cereal. She straightens the collar of his coat before he leaves for school. She has gone back to listening to Tallis in the afternoons, a remarkable recording by the Tallis Scholars, and as she listens something like a kite string reaches down and pulls at her thoughts, which are not quite ready to be thoughts. It might be that she's putting her own heart beside itself, making comparisons. What does it mean to be better or best?

One of the new, young music gurus, writing in the weekend papers, believes Tallis is actually a better composer than Byrd. What had been considered simple in his work is now thought of as subtle. What struck earlier critics as primitive is really a form of understated sophistication. Perhaps these judgments boil down to mere fashion. Or perhaps the recent Tallis biography has upped his reputation.

Imagine a girl just twenty-one years old—I'm aware that I probably should say "young woman," but there is so much girlishness in her face and in the way she sets off from home each morning, running a quarter of a mile to the Tube station, swinging her leather satchel at her side. She is probably in love or at least drawn to the possibility of love. Undoubtedly she thinks about the new clenched knot of ardour in her chest, thinks of it all day long, coming and going to her classes, while seated at the piano and also at the harpsichord, which she has recently taken up. Her head may be swarming with Latin, with choral efforts, with the rising and falling and patterning of sound, but her body presses against this new, rapturous apparition.

Then one day, late in May, she meets a young man. They collide on the Tube, not the most romantic of venues. This man is awkward, he has holes in his pockets, he is ungainly in his appearance. He is really rather ordinary, as a matter of fact, immersed as he is in the drainage capability of compacted gravel, and so lacking in perception that he will never understand why she agreed to have a coffee with him instead of attending her class. He's a lad, that's all, just another face, though he flatters himself that she sees something in him. Why, otherwise, does she go to the cinema with him on that first afternoon, and then out for fish and chips, and later, only a week later, does she end up in his flat, in his bed?

Why does she marry him, him of all people? Why do they buy a house in a semi-respectable area of London, produce three quite nice children, take holidays in Scotland or else in Yorkshire where her mother lives? And why—another question altogether—when her book on Tallis is launched at a large cocktail buffet, and her publisher suggests that she write about William Byrd, does she shake her head "no"?

Let someone else do Byrd, her look said on that occasion.

But now, one year later she's rethinking the matter. Yes, Byrd. Why not?

The system of temperament in the family shifts once again, and so does the onward allotment of time. As before, this woman rises early each day, but this time to put together her notes on William Byrd, the divine William Byrd, who seems suddenly in danger of being eclipsed by his renowned teacher and mentor.

She allows the house to fill up with dust and clutter. When her husband drops a kiss on the back of her neck, she shakes her hair impatiently. Her word processor sends out blinding windows of authority. She's busy, she's preoccupied, she's committing an act of redemption. A choir of ten thousand voices sings inside her head. No wonder she's been looking at her husband lately with an odd, assessing, measuring clarity.

More and more he tries to stay out of her way, and more and more he refers to himself in the third person. He's an ordinary man, no one to make a fuss over. He insists on that. Nevertheless he finds himself opening his ears to the new music that's overtaken the house.

Soup du Jour

EVERYONE IS COMING OUT these days for the pleasures of ordinary existence. Sunsets. Dandelions. Fencing in the backyard and staying home. "The quotidian is where it's at," Herb Rhinelander wrote last week in his nationwide syndicated column. "People are getting their highs on the level roller coaster of everydayness, dipping their daily bread in the soup of common delight and simple sensation."

A ten-year-old child is sent to the corner store to buy a bunch of celery, and this small isolated event with its sounds, smells, and visual texture yields enough footage for a feature film. A woman bending over her embroidery pauses to admire the hitherto unremarked beauty of her thimble, its cozy steel blue utility, its dimpled perfection. A walker stumbles over a fallen log and apprehends with piercing suddenness the crumbling racy aroma of rotted wood, how the smell of history rises from such natural decay, entropy's persistent perfume, more potent than the strongest hallucinogen and free for the taking. Nowadays people ill in their beds draw courage from the shapeliness of their bedposts, the plangent software of cut flowers, Hall-mark cards, or knitted covers for their boiled eggs, and such eggs! Such yellowness of yolk! Such complementary wrap and gloss of white.

Everywhere adolescent girls stare into ditches where rainwater collects and mirrors the colours of passion; their young men study the labels of soup cans, finding therein a settled, unbreakable belief in their own self-sufficiency. The ordinary has become extraordinary. All at once—it seems to have happened in the last hour, the last ten minutes—there is no stone, shrub, chair, or door that does not offer arrows of implicit meaning or promises of epiphany.

Only think of Ronald Graham-Sutcliffe in his Dorset garden among his damasks and gallicas. Modern roses do not interest Mr. Graham-Sutcliffe. They remind him of powder puffs, and of periods of his life that now strike him as being unnecessarily complicated. He still feels a stern duty to weigh the suffering in every hour, but this duty is closely followed by the wish to obliterate it. He pulls on his Wellingtons in the morning, every morning now that he's retired, and does a quick stiff-legged patrol among his fertile borders. He locks his hands behind his body, the better to keep his balance as he moves forward with his old man's dangerous toppling assurance. Times have changed; he no longer counts the numbers of new buds or judges the quality of colour. He's gone beyond all that. Now, standing at the middle tide of old age, it's quite enough to take in a single flower's slow, filmic unfolding. One rose, he sees, stands for all roses, one petal drifting to the soft ground matches the inevitable erosion of his own essential unimportance. This is natural harmony, this is the greatest possible happiness, he says to himself, then draws back as though the thought has come from someone more vulgar than himself.

He savours too his morning tea with its twirl of white milk. And his bedtime whisky; now that he's allowed only one a day, he's learned to divide the measure into an infinite number of sips, each sip marking off a minute on his tongue and a tingle of heat in his folded gut. At the end of the day, hot soapy bathwater laps against the thinness of ectomorphic legs, surely not his legs, these jointed shanks with their gleam of Staffordshire pearl, though he acknowledges distant cousinage. Afloat on the surface are his pinkish testicles, clustered like the roe of a largish lake fish, yes, his, definitely his, undeniably his, but nothing to make a fuss over. Not anymore. He is a man for whom ambition has been more vital than achievement, fleshly volume more imperative than mastery. He sees this clearly, and has no further expectations, none that count in the real world. His army years, his time in the colonial service, his difficulty with women (one in particular), his throat full of unconfessed longings—all have come to rest in a large white porcelain tub and a warm towel waiting, folded beautifully, over a chromium rail.

Mrs. Graham-Sutcliffe, Molly to her friends, is seated on a small green sofa in a Dorset sitting room, a book open on her lap. Lamplight throws a spume of whiteness around her which is more flattering than she can possibly know. She is memorizing French verbs in an attempt to give meaning to her life. Naturally she favours those regular, self-engrossed verbs—*manger, penser, réfléchir, dormir*—that attach to the small unalarming segments of her daily existence. She loves her daily existence, which includes, although she hasn't thought to acknowledge it, the pale arc of lamplight and the hooting of owls reaching her through the open window. Entering the various doorways of present, imperfect, future anterior, and subjunctive, she perceives and cherishes the overlapping of one moment with the next, the old unstoppable, unfoolable nature of time itself.

Exuberant and healthy, except for the usual grindings and twinges, she has a hearty respect for those paragraphs in a full life that need reworking. As a young child she was attacked by a madwoman on a London omnibus. The woman, who was later arrested and sent to an asylum, pulled a package of lamb chops from a leather bag and hurled them with all her strength at young Molly's straw boater. Something about the child, the yellowness of her hair, the eager wet shine of her eyes, had excited the woman's rage. Molly's hat was knocked askew. She was struck on the left cheek and ear, and the precise shape and weight of the blow have been stamped on her memory.

For a year or two she woke from sleep trembling and pressing her hands up against her face and emitting little muffled yelps of terror. In another epoch, in another sort of family, she might have been sent to an analyst in an attempt to erase the wound. Instead she learned to nurse the incident along, to touch it up with a blush of comedy. She has by now related the story to hundreds of friends and acquaintances, smoothing out its strangeness in the telling, assigning herself a cameo role of amused passivity. The story ripples with light. There is something, after all, more intrinsically droll about a packet of lamb chops than, say, a brick. Lamb chops ascend more readily to myth, as witness the greaseproof paper that has long since slipped away and the butcher's twine. Bone, flesh, and gristle, and a border of hard yellow fat, are caught in midflight aboard a rather charming period conveyance, and there the image rests, shivering amid the most minor of vibrations and eliciting throttled laughter from Molly Graham-Sutcliffe's many good-natured friends.

In the same gregarious, self-mocking manner, she has transformed other, similarly seismic nightmares into the currency of the mundane and mild—her dozens of inconvenient household moves over the years, an agonizing childbirth that yielded a stillborn lump with a cord around its neck, the spreading, capricious arthritis in her elbows and knees, and Mr. Graham-Sutcliffe's occasional indiscretions, one in particular. There is a verb, she's found, to match every unpardonable act, and every last verb can be broken down until it becomes as faultless and ordinary and innocently inquisitive as that little sleepy English infinitive: to be.

And now, with Mr. Graham-Sutcliffe still in his bathwater and his wife Molly on her green sofa, nodding a little over her French grammar and feeling a slight chill from the open window, it seems as good a time as any to leave Dorset behind, thousands of miles behind, and move on to the other side of the world.

But there is a chill too in the city of Montreal where, with the five-hour time difference, it is late afternoon on a breezy spring day. A woman by the name of Heather Hotchkiss, age forty, is standing in the kitchen of a suburban bungalow, stirring a pot of homemade soup. She is the owner/manager of a laundromat in nearby Les Ormes de Bois and finds after the long working day, Mondays in particular, that there is nothing so soothing, so cheering, as the chopping, stirring, seasoning, and tasting that are part of the art of soup making. In her right hand she grasps a wooden spoon. Its handle, worn smooth by many washings, provides a frisson of added pleasure, as does the rising steam with its uplifting fragrance of onion, carrot, garlic, and cabbage. She stirs and sniffs like the practical-minded ordinary woman she feels herself to be. The diced potato and celery will be added only during the last half hour of cooking in order to preserve their more fragile flavour and texture.

This much she learned from her mother, who undoubtedly learned it from her mother and so forth ad infinitum. The mysteries of soup making are ancient. You would have to go back a thousand years, perhaps further, to discover its intricacies and logic, whereas you would have to go back only ten or twelve years to uncover the portion of Heather Hotchkiss's life that she dissolves so expediently, so unconsciously, in her steaming, wholesome vegetable brews.

Ten years ago people in the movies still smoked and laughed deep within their throats. The world was extravagant and feckless. Nevertheless churches, at least in the larger English market towns, were locked up for the first time against vandals. Heads were shaved or dyed blue. Lovers gave each other flashy gifts such as diamond cuff-links or microwave ovens, bought on the never-never. Ten years ago the pleasures of everyday existence were known only to a handful. Everyone else, Heather Hotchkiss included, wanted more.

More of everything, more risk, more moments of excited intimacy, more pain, more heightened eroticism, more self-destruction, more high-kicking desire, more altered states of consciousness, more sensual fulfillment, more forgiveness, more capitulation, more lingering surrender, more rapturous loss of breath, more unhealed grief, more hours pressed into the service of ecstasy, more air, more weather, more surfaces to touch, more damage, more glimpses of heaven. Ten or twelve years ago Heather Hotchkiss, in love with Ronald Graham-Sutcliffe, a married man old enough to be her father, would have hooted at the simple delight of soup making, but this is where time has delivered her, across an ocean, to the suburb of a large North American city where she is the proprietor of a well-run business with a reasonable profit margin, in good health but with greying hair, bent over a stainless-steel cauldron of bubbling soup. She also knits, swims at the Y, reads books on gardening, practises meditation, and takes her son Simon for weekend walks on Mount Royal.

Simon, aged ten, is in love this spring with the cracks of sidewalks, their furrowed darkness and decay and their puzzling microcosmic promise. The earth opens, the earth closes; the scars are straight, uniform, and accessible—or are they? Sometimes he sees the spreading stain of a burgeoning ant colony, sometimes surprise tufts of coarse grass or weeds. He never steps on a crack, never. Over the winter his legs have grown to such an extent that he can dodge the tricky cracks while pretending indifference, looking skyward, whistling, humming, day-dreaming, and, more than anything else, counting. He is a ritual counter. There are ten provinces in his country. There are 34 children in his class at school, 107 iron spikes in the schoolyard fence, and 322 squares of pavement between his house and the corner store where his mother often sends him on errands. He is firmly under the spell of these sidewalk sections, these islands, compelled to count them again and again, ever watchful for variation or trickery. Sometimes, not often, he is inattentive and finds himself one or two numbers out. Then he feels a temporary diminishment of his powers and an attack of gooseflesh on his neck and arms. He knows his life depends on the memorizing of the immediate, proximate world.

But today he concentrates so hard on the task of counting squares that he arrives in front of the grocery forgetting what has brought him here. His mother sent him, true. She gave him a five-dollar bill. A single item is required, but what? He is ready to die with the shame of it. He cannot return home empty-handed and he cannot enter the store and engage the pity of Mr. Singh, the owner, who would immediately telephone his mother and ask what it is she requires.

He freezes, hugs the points of his elbows, thinking hard, bringing the whole of his ten years into play. Today is Monday. The day when his mother is most inclined towards soup making. He pictures the two bowls of soup, one for her, one for him, side by side on the smooth pine table. He sees clearly the red woven placemats and the gleaming spoons with their running banners of light, and then the various coloured vegetables floating in a peppery broth.

He takes a breath, pokes a stick between the squares of concrete, and begins the process of elimination. Not carrots, not onions, not potatoes. As he strikes these items from the familiar list, he experiences the same ponderable satisfaction he finds in naming such other absences as father or brother or uncle, always imagining these gaps to be filled with a leather-fresh air of possibility, just around the corner, just five minutes out of reach.

At that moment the word *celery* arrives, fully shaped, extracted cleanly from the black crack in the pavement, the final crack (as luck would have it) before the three smooth cement steps that lead up to the sill of the corner store. The boy's gratitude is thunderous. He almost stumbles under the punishment of it, thinking how he will remember it all his life, even when he is old and forgetful and has given up his obsession with counting. He says it out loud, *celery*, transforming the word into a brilliantly coloured balloon that swims and rises and overcomes the tiny confines of the ordinary everyday world to which, until this moment, he has been condemned.

Invention

———

M Y GRANDMOTHER, as everyone knows, was the inventor of the steering-wheel muff.

It was born of love. She was a woman who adored her young husband, she doted on him, and her invention was a tribute to that love. Never a driver herself, she worried about the way my grandfather's gloved hands slipped on the steering wheel in the winter—ours is a country with a long and bitter winter season, icy roads, danger at every turn. When Grandfather was forced to remove his gloves in order to secure a firmer grip on the wheel, his knuckles quickly turned white with cold. She was pained by the sight of that whiteness, and moved to do what she could.

It took her a single afternoon to crochet her first model, her prototype, you might say. It proved less than satisfactory, however, since it offered little purchase on the smooth surface of their Buick's steering wheel. What to do? She looked around and discovered another kind of wool with improved adhesive properties, wool that was imported from a region on the coast of west Ireland where the sheep graze on certain regional sedges and beach grass, there being an absence of ordinary turf. She also experimented with an elastic edging, then lined the "glove," as she called it in the early days, with a strip of gathered chamois.

My grandfather, a lover of gadgets, was delighted. He called it his steering wheel "chapeau," and demonstrated its usefulness to his colleagues. Soon my grandmother was busy making her little hand-wrought coverings for their many friends. She tried flannel, corduroy, fur, velvet, suede, burlap, all with greater or lesser success, and gave away her various models as hospitality gifts or stocking stuffers. One of these friends wrote her a thank-you note saying: "My steering wheel is now snug in its beautiful winter muff," and the official term—*muff*—was born, just weeks before she hired four helpers, women recruited from the Alice House for Unwed Mothers, and set up a workshop in the attic of her home on Russell Road.

Money began to trickle in, then became rivers of money, especially when she introduced her famous faux-leopard muff, which became the signature for all that was chic, young, adventurous, and daring.

People were surprised at how she threw herself into the muff enterprise. A small factory was built north of the city, which she launched by breaking a ginger-ale bottle across the workers' gate, and this moment was immortalized in a Pathé newsreel. (You can if you look carefully make out the blurred image of my grandfather, smiling proudly from the sidelines.) Other factories were put into operation, Cincinnati, Manchester, Hong Kong. To this day production has never quite managed to keep up with demand, which is more than you can say about other products. The market had been waiting, it seemed, for just such a utilitarian accessory. She in her housedress and apron, she who had been timid about speaking into her own telephone, was interviewed more than once on the radio about the benefits of the muff, which not only warmed a cold surface but brought coolness—in Arizona, New Mexico, California—to the problem of a *hot* steering wheel. Who would have thought it—that an object this simple could bring consumer satisfaction to so many.

Except to my grandfather, of course, whose spirits withered as the wheel-muff empire grew.

In his later years he went back to the cold, rigid bone of an undressed steering wheel. A serious driver, he maintained, cherished the direct touch of the hand on the steering apparatus, the control, the feeling of resonating with the working engine, of being part of the mechanism itself and not separated from it by a piece of superfluous "fluff." Almost every day he could be seen driving erratically up and down Russell Road, grasping his naked steering wheel in his hard old hands, his flesh sealed against comfort. This went on for years, not that my grand-mother paid the least attention. By that time they were living apart.

Invention is a curious gift, and may well be over-credited. Invention is not so much about creation as "find-ing out"; the word's Latin origin says it clearly, *invenire*, meaning to come upon. My grandmother would have defined it, initially anyway, as making do, improving, stumbling across—but then success made her dizzy, then arrogant, and then she became "an inventor."

Just think of how many times that woman went to court to protect her patents! Think of how sternly she dealt with the Cincinnati strike. Where did she find the strength to confront public attention? And all the while her tem-perament grew discoloured, so that she forgot utterly that long-ago moment when she was a young woman, passion-ately, tenderly in love with her handsome new husband, glancing across the width of the car at his gloved hands slipping on the wheel and thinking: what can I do to show my ardour?

It was quite otherwise for Fulham-Cooper, my famed precursor through my mother's side of the family, a late sixteenth-century grammarian whose blood I am happy to claim. Fulham-Cooper did not, of course, start out as a grammarian, but was, as his name announces, a cooper, one who earned his living by making and repairing barrels in a sleepy corner of rural England. He was greatly gifted in his trade, however, and had a head for business. *And* he was literate, something of an anomaly in that era. In time he was able to employ two or three assistants, later as many as twenty. A regional map of the period shows that his village eventually bore his name: Fulhamton. It might be thought that such a man would direct his inventive energy towards improving the traditional barrel or cask, but instead my ancestor invented the hyphen.

As you know, much mediaeval writing came down to us enjambed on the page, one word running smack into the next. Those monks sweating over their manuscripts and devoted to the preservation of sacred texts, gave only minimal thought to how difficult they made the act of reading. What good fortune, then, that Simon the Wise (no relation, I'm sorry to say) invented the word-space. He was widely celebrated for this device, and justly so, in my opinion, though a space, like a zero, may seem at first a negative triumph, mere air masquerading as substance.

Well, we know differently today. Emptiness has weight; absence gestures at meaning. A doorway is privileged over an actual door in its usefulness and even its beauty—to give a homely example. A caesura locks a poem into a grid of understanding; a silence distinguishes speech from speech and thought from thought.

After the discovery of the word-space came that spirited novelty the period or full stop, a collaborative invention by a pair of unmarried Jutland sisters, both skilled embroiderers, in need of a stitch (they used a French knot) to conclude or accent a line of scripture running along the length of a linen altar cloth, a treasure which is now preserved at the Victoria and Albert Museum, its precious threads disintegrating between sheets of glass, but available to public view if one applies to the curator in writing.

The cryptic comma was, I like to think, devised by one Brother Alphonse, a very distant cousin on my paternal grandfather's side, who was also known for his fine woodcuts and his habit of near-continuous prayer. One day, as he was lost in meditation, the nib of his pen slipped downward and sideways, and instead of depositing a fine, precise dot on his sheet of precious parchment, he left a curled worm of ambiguity, which he recognized at once as a sacred pause, a resting place during which time he might breathe out his thanks to God for the richness of his blessings, and prepare his next imprecation. *Let me be free in my thoughts, let me be clean in my acts, let me never lose connection with the holy bonds between me and Thee, and the everlasting earth, amen, amen, amen, ad infinitum…*

My own ancestor's invention of the hyphen derives directly from his barrel-making skills. Consider the barrel, which is nothing more, after all, than a circle of bent staves held together by an iron hoop. The simple hoop connects what is otherwise unconnectable, since the barrel-maker's wooden strips long to spring apart.

A hyphen takes on the same function. A diacritical mark of great simplicity, it joins what is similar and also what is disjunctive. Two words may be read as one, a case of compounding meaning and doubling force, but this horizontal bar, requiring only a sweet, single stroke of the pen, divides as well as marries. How clever of my kinsman to know that successful inventions are both functional and elegant. Aesthetically, the hyphen is superior to the slash, you will agree, and it makes a set of parentheses look like crude homemade fencing.

Fulham-Cooper, later Sir Fulham-Cooper, may have been a genius, or he may simply have "fallen upon" his useful contribution. I am proud to come from a long line of inventors, but I recognize, at the same time, that invention is random and accidental. For instance: someone discovered one idle afternoon that a loop of plastic tubing will defy gravity if gyrated rapidly around the human body. Someone else, in another slot of time, noticed that a mixture of potassium nitrate, charcoal, and sulphur will create a new substance which is highly explosive. Some unsung hero invented the somersault, not to mention the cartwheel. Other people—through carelessness or luck or distraction or necessity—invented keys, chairs, wheels, thermometers, and the theory of evolution.

As I say, the spirit of invention seems rooted in my own family history. The proof is there. I have tracked this genetic facility carefully, and friends of mine have even been kind enough to suggest that I might qualify as a professional genealogist, especially since I have managed, finally, to document my family tree all the way back to Titus the Shepherd—one of my Greek-speaking forebears. His invention, though he himself was a lazy young man, and naturally was thought by his parents to be a wastrel, altered the entire nature of human consciousness.

It happened late on a summer afternoon. Titus, a shepherd like his father and grandfather, was bored. The sheep were stupid with heat that day, slow in their movements, and abjectly obedient. None strayed. Instead they huddled miserably in the shade of a small fig tree, unmoving. There was no breeze, no cloud overhead, nothing to break through the emptiness in Titus's head.

He waved his staff in the direction of another shepherd on another hill, a greeting of sorts, anything to interrupt his ennui, but met with no response. It would be hours yet before he might return home, eat his mother's soup of onions and fennel, and endure his father's bitter complaints, and another hour or two before he would be able to take refuge in his bed.

All day long he yearned for his bed. There he at once fell asleep and dreamed, and his dreams made him happy.

When he was a very small boy he asked his father what this thing was that happened at night. How did the night stories enter the house and find their way behind his eyes with their colours and shapes and drama? Such richness. "These are dreams," he was told. "Everyone is given dreams."

Sometimes his dreams frightened him. He was chased by a bear and eaten. His mother fell ill. He was naked, shamed. He felt a terrible hunger, a thirst. But even these visions of tragedy brought their gifts, their excitement. They carried movement, possibility, a raising of the blood. Furthermore their shadow would soon shift sideways, he knew this, and make space for the good dreams he had come to depend upon; even their decaying presence offered the promise of the next night and the next dream story. The world could be made and unmade in this way. It could go on forever.

The most skilled genealogist—and I am only an amateur, as I have said—cannot give an account of another's dreams. Titus has left no records himself, but it is established that he was healthy and able. And one can easily guess what a young man's dreams might consist of. Feats of courage, no doubt. Saving one of his father's lambs, for instance, and earning extravagant public tribute. And surely he would dream of women, young women, old women, their clean skins and secret clefts. Their songs and offerings and quick, dark-eyed glances. And the heaving of a sudden rhythmic rapture that quickly emptied itself and began again, again, and again, played out in the darkness, a story unfolded and made brilliant.

But for now there are no dreams to distract and amuse.

The sun, he notices, is still almost straight overhead. The sheep make their soft, useless noises of appetite and suffering in their hotly lit circle. It will be hours before Titus will be in his cool bed, dreaming. The thought is unbearable, unbearable.

To offer himself a measure of solace, and to pass the time, he begins to dream about dreaming. It is as though he has opened a small, previously unknown door in his head. He does not dare shut his eyes, of course, for his father's small flock is his responsibility; he doesn't dare let even one sheep out of sight. He breathes in and out, and at that moment feels a dividing of consciousness. He exists in two places at once, stubbornly rooted to this dull hillside, solitary, dimly aware, but at the same time he feels himself carried into a story of splendour and bravery. There is music, vibrancy. His spine stretches. The grip on consciousness is firm, yet a woman is walking towards him, a beautiful woman with a thin band of gold around her left wrist. She is reaching out her slender arms. What can she be saying? He can scarcely believe what he hears: she is chanting his name. Titus. I've found you.

A distortion of time occurs, though he isn't sure whether it is elongated or shortened. A dozen strands and subplots creep into the dream story. Opportunities for bold deeds multiply, and he hears himself named on a role of honour: Brave Titus, Noble Titus. Circling the crowded scenes of action are softer lights, alternative arrangements, where a vague beauty presses and offers ease. Its glaze covers the hillside, even the flanks of the standing sheep and the pathetic little fig tree bent against the air.

For a moment it seems the vision is about to collapse, but he manages to draw it back to life. Onward. A new, freshly furnished story rumbles into view with its defining line of phosphorescence. And next...and then...and finally...

The rest of Titus's day passes in what seems a moment. In no time he is ducking through the doorway of his parents' house, where the smell of soup greets him. He can't wait to tell them what he has discovered. He makes them sit down and listen carefully. He can dream in the daytime as well as at night, he says. He can dream with his eyes wide open, never for a minute losing his concentration on the silly sheep.

"A day-dream," his father says, full of wonder. "I must try this out for myself."

"You have chanced upon something of great value," his mother says, and she touches his shoulder with respect, understanding at once that this new form of consciousness will bring creativity and salvation and grace where before nothing but dullness had been.

No wonder I feel fortunate to be a humble leaf on my family tree. This tree thrives, its energy flows into the world making its offerings and inventions. The fact that I myself lack inventive fervour is not a cause for sadness, you must believe me; I know perfectly well that if the spirit of invention were too widely distributed, the world would implode.

Some of us are needed who merely keep the historical record. We count, we describe, we make our small forays into the archives. We keep track of our findings.

We interpret, we analyse, we speculate. And sometimes we risk our small emendations. Perhaps this too is part of invention.

Death of
an Artist

THE OLD MAN IS DEAD.

At least he appears to be dead, lying there, *nested* there in oaky repose, relaxed under a demi-coverlet, the coffin lid tufted and ribboned and stuck with flowers. People shuffle by and stare down at him, remarking how like himself he looks. His last disguise.

In fact, his face is fleshier, angrier, than it appeared on the screen, knobbed and prehistoric with its thug's nose, long bony white-tipped ears, thickish lips, and a tongue that now and then deceived him on the tube, wagging and twitching while he thrust about for one of those Anglo-Gallic witticisms of his, Oscar Wilde with a dash of maple syrup, always playing the role, the wimpled satyr. Now you see him, now you don't.

No one knew him, really knew him. The history of his choleric, odd, furiously unproductive, and thoroughly unsatisfying life is most clearly set out in his diaries, eight plump volumes, but difficult to decipher because of the red crayon he affected, and the cheap lined schoolboy paper. These "undiaries," as he himself once called them, are best read in reverse, that is, you should begin with the final entry and work your way backwards.

Never mind the smiting, toxic scrawl. Begin. Observe him, then, at age eighty-eight, the infant's tongue lolling and speaking his need. His weepy red script holds the glare of old regrets and fresh insights. "This has been the most remarkable day of my life," he writes after making his desperate and theatrical journey, actually hoisting himself onto a train one June morning and going back to that country crossroads where he was born.

As a pilgrimage it was heroic, he with his tick-tocky heart and plugged lungs, playing the hoary sage, the native son. He required two canes, if you remember, to move himself along, wheezing and wiping the tears from his eyes. That was a side of him that perhaps only Emily knew: his sentimentality, his foundering in the folds of memory, those long sighs and leaky snuffles, just barely audible in his broadcasts.

The two canes, of course, were part of his getup, his self-relishment. In his left hand he grasped the aluminum rod, spare and modern, government-issue; in his right, the burnished sycamore wand owned by his putative grand-father, former choir member and townsman. Between these two symbolic props he balanced himself, blinking at the camera, a tottery old paradox, eliciting sympathy while projecting scorn, disdainful of the particular but committed to the whole. Wink, blink. "Well, yes," he barked into the microphone. The sun shone down. His beard was hand-somely stiff and speckled. It was said that before his public appearances he shampooed it with the yolk of an egg, and that he considered it a mark of virility, though probably only Emily was entirely privy to this remark.

His seventies were his best decade, when, as he himself said, he was most nearly himself. The pension helped, also the milder climate. Often he strolled in the park of an after-noon, for the sheer pleasure of its symmetrical flower-beds and settled statuary. During the whole of this era his only shred of posture was a Victorian parasol, printed with poppies, bought for ninepence in a north London market. "Forgive this artifice," he said to a reporter who asked why he carried it. "But one must protect one's self from one's self." The same reporter inquired as to his political views (and he admitted to a rather filthy vision of the future). And about his costive use of semicolons; and his opinions on his fellow "artistes"; and why he now referred to himself as "one." A photographer captured him forever, standing by a singing fountain, his parasol raised, fending off not sun but rain, and uttering one of those off-the-cuffers which we now know to have been laboriously prepared and memorized and repeated. "One is ultimately faithful to one's infidelities," he twice uttered.

So much for his seventies, his sun-strewn seventies, when even Emily appeared to be taken in by his little affinities with nature, his ornithological potherings, his urban botanizing. "*Les mauvaises herbes*," he sniffed, returning home from his afternoon strolls and tucking away the parasol for another day.

In his sixties he was in his full strength, or, to quote from his "anti-journal," at the zenith of his weakness. He roared and whimpered, bellowed and bled. It was said he perfected the grunt. Made it his. He bought a ruff to wear around his neck and a pair of tights for his not-yet-completely-withered shanks. Emily has left a suitable account of this period, in which she submits her theory of possible drug dependency, Valium to be precise. Just to see him before the medicine cabinet was to feel an unstitching of certainty. Chemical tranquility brought an instant alias, transported him effortlessly into his other selves. When he drooped and sighed, he did so with authenticity and vigour. She worried, though, about his predilection for Turkish towelling (the term *terry cloth* was anathema to him) and speculated with her usual perspicacity that a thwarted sexuality was at the core. He received during this decade several mysterious phone calls, generally late in the morning, and worked tirelessly on his telephone mannerisms, cupping the receiver in a malevolent fashion, and glancing upwards at the ceiling tile as though the ultimate tabulation of those acoustical squares might bring about the onslaught of popular acceptance—something he both courted and feared. He was, Emily says, an afternoon aristocrat and a twilight prole. Suppers he took in silence, like a monk.

His fifties were another matter. Some biographers suggest that it was during this period that his masquerade became the most elaborate and self-defoliating. He once, for instance, borrowed (stole) a child's wagon, filled it with bedding plants, and went door to door through the western suburbs, offering his wares, gratis, to anyone kind enough to accept. No one did; doors were slammed; he wrote about this experience later in his "neo-diaries" (vol. 6), calling it a national disgrace and a symptom of global paranoia. It was not a happy time. More than once he threatened retirement—"one wearies, one wearies"—but something hammy in his thundering brushed close to truth. In short, he made the mistake of becoming picturesque, forgetting that subterfuge requires more than consistency.

In his mid-forties he fell in love. Emily, of course, a case of feminine predicament and masculine opportunity or perhaps the reverse. May and December, one of those doomed unions, but one that was also blessed. "Entirely glandular," he blustered to his public, "and also deeply spiritual." They were snapped in a discount store by the pa-

parazzi, she pushing a cart with her look of benighted lustre and he playing the fool with a clutch of credit cards. At
the checkout the girls winked, but at the bank there was
trouble. He was forced into a radical reassessment during
which his persona received a touch-up job, almost a replat-
ing. "I am at heart an average person," he sincerely
announced at a small ad hoc press conference in the vicinity of his neighbourhood.

In his thirties—his chimera period, he called it—he was
a sought-after dinner guest, and it was his habit, during this
epoch, to carry a set of car keys in his hand. They gave him
a sweet jingle, a certain cachet, becoming a trademark or, if
you like, a kind of statement to the world. These keys, he
seemed to say, spell evanescence. Transience. Fleeting grace.

An apocryphal story from the same period has him
travelling about town carrying a mandolin, the origins of
which are unknown but much disputed. On buses and
streetcars, generally sitting towards the front, he rested this
instrument across his knees in a lateral position, and frequently tapped its varnished frame with his fingers, creating
a rhythmic effect.

And of course there is his toque, acquired in his twen-
ties, that remarkable chapeau of knitted wool with its
famed double tassel, worn throughout his life, tilted over
his left or right ear. Often, once or twice a day, he lifted his
hand and touched it lightly in a kind of ironic salute to the
unhatted universe. "Hey, do you sleep in that thing?" a

cheeky radio reporter once asked him, stopping him in the middle of his midday walk.

Throughout his teenage years he visited, not surprisingly, country churches and sat beneath any number of trees. "Were you starting to get self-aware during this period?" is a question often posed, and the probable answer is: perhaps. Certainly he was assembling the philosophy of non-merciless adaptation we find today limned in his "crypto-diaries." His around-the-house costume in those teen years consisted of a rough cotton robe (forerunner of his Turkish towelling period?) and a pair of comfortable slippers said to have been presented to him by his mother on his thirteenth birthday. A coming-of-age gesture, perhaps. Ceremony has always figured importantly in his rubric, and a pair of slippers at such an auspicious age cannot have been without meaning.

No serious person pays attention to his childhood, he is said to have said, though evidence points to the contrary. A small set of building blocks, for instance, cannot be discounted. And a spinning top. *Spinning*! A silver cup with his name misspelled at the lip. And of course the red crayon, without which his name would be only a name and his life less than a life.

"I am utterly alone," he wrote (in red) across the top of the final page.

There has been no mention of an inquiry.

The Next
Best Kiss

—

TODD AND SANDY HAD been friends for just a few weeks, and Sandy knew they were about to say good-bye to each other.

This thing between them was an episode taking place on a small screen. A mini-flick, as Todd would say, a scenario, a sketch. A million words had flown by, but nothing had been promised or declared, and Sandy could sense the way she and Todd were using each other up minute by minute, one talky voice drinking the other dry.

Both of them loved to talk—or, more accurately, they felt compelled to talk. A hyperverbal compulsion was what they shared, way up there on the glottal thermometer, and that was putting it kindly. This talkiness might have been genetic, or it might have been what was expected of them. They were both professors, he on the West Coast, she on the East; she was in history, he was in sociology/film studies/cultural exegesis. ("Professor of et cetera"—that was one of Todd's little jokes on himself, almost his only joke.)

Friends introduced them to each other at the reception that launched the 1998 Darlington Conference, in Detroit, devoted to the subject of *fin de siècle* crisis. Todd gave a paper titled "End of the Self," about the instability of the self, the self as the sum of incalculable misunderstandings, and the selfishness of even claiming a self. Todd confided to Sandy that the text for his talk might eventually find its way into the *New York Review of Books*, although the editors were asking for substantial changes, which Todd was questioning—and quite rightly, he said.

Sandy presented an afternoon seminar, "Diatribe and Discourse in the Twenty-first Century," prophetic in its pronouncements, spacy, brilliant (she hoped), loaded with allusive arrows (Lacan in particular), and followed by a vigorous Q-and-A session, with Todd, seated out there in the audience, contributing a number of thoughtful comments and reservations.

"He's an asshole," Sandy's colleague Chloe said afterwards.

"No," Sandy countered, "not an asshole. Just an ass. One of those silly, old-fashioned asses." She said this with a fond smile, all the muscles in her face and body relaxed for once. "Like our fathers were. Or our uncles. Total asses."

"He talks in clauses, Sandy. You're not supposed to *talk* in clauses. And especially not with semicolons intervening. I can hear those semicolons coming at me. Little squash balls hitting the wall."

Sandy was still smiling; she couldn't help herself. "There's no law against semicolons."

Since their first meeting Sandy's jaws and Todd's jaws had not stopped moving. They had a verbal Ping-Pong game going, a monsoon, unstoppable. Sexually, they seemed to belong to the same nation—the strenuous, the informed, the adventurous, the currently unattached. On the other hand, anyone could see that they were far from being matched linguistically. Todd's ruminations tended to be speculative. Sandy's narrative.

For example: "We've probably said farewell to the world of sermons and to the clenched piety of holy pilgrimages," Todd said in his lecture, question marks hovering over his words like a jangle of surprised coat hangers. "We may soon be surrendering our sacred objects and perhaps the practice of prayer—even the notion of prayer."

"You seem to be hedging your bets a bit," Sandy told him after the presentation, not wanting to smother him in blanket approval—it was too soon for that. "The use of 'probably' and 'perhaps' and 'may be' and so on."

She had learned that women are obliged to interrupt

their own discourse for the discourse of others, using standard probes and thrusts and "sincere" attempts at interrogation—the same strategies their mothers once used.

"It's ironic, but the *probable* now holds more force than the *certain*," Todd told her mysteriously, cradling her in his arms that first night, stretching his neck and kissing the tender place where her hairline met the back of her neck. "Because it more and more appears to be self-evident that nothing is really conclusive."

"You could be right," Sandy said. She was having trouble with her breathing and wasn't sure whether the cause was emotional or physical. Todd had a large, solid body. She appreciated its weight (she had been a long time between men and their bodily heft), but at the same time she felt vulnerable being pinned down like this.

"Everything's smaller now," Todd continued, minutely shifting his body. "Our idea of love is smaller. Our friendships are smaller."

"Yes," she said. "Emphatically. Why, back in the nineteenth century love was big stuff. As big as those balloons people used to ride around the world in. Now it's more like the kind of grit that gets left behind in your jeans pocket."

"Yeah, sort of," Todd said.

He listened politely enough to her account of childbirth, the moment eleven years earlier when Jenny burst from her womb, as wet and compacted as a supermarket chicken with her folded limbs and tight whorls of dark hair, but Sandy, who liked to make a terse drama of her birth event, could tell that Todd's thoughts were elsewhere.

His eyes were squeezed shut, and he had gone suddenly critical in a pedagogical way that was quickly becoming familiar; his arms were around her, but in her imagination he was standing a few feet away, holding a clipboard in his hand and a microphone to his lips, analysing her narrative structure and syntax.

"Womb?" he murmured. "Now, that's a somewhat romantic, nineteenth-century word to bring into a modern clinical procedure."

"It's not clinical at all," Sandy was about to say, but Todd started telling her about his automobile accident in Mexico—Baja California, to be exact—as though there were some connection between birth and highway injury.

Perhaps there was, the cooler half of her brain bleeped this possibility. Human tissue. Tearing and bleeding. Sudden intervention. She had noticed that people who have been in car crashes always get around to these stories fast. They love their accidents. Road disasters are like five-star movies in their lives, the only time they've been allowed to be major actors. "They had to pry open the door to get me out," Todd was saying. "The ambulance attendant kept saying it was a miracle I was still breathing." His voice went rough and shy with remembrance.

"It must have been terrible."

"Worse than terrible."

"How much worse?" She hoped she didn't sound as though she were mocking him.

"What?"

"I mean, how do we measure these things?"

"Do you always have to measure everything?"

A good question—or was it? "I suppose," she said slowly, easing his elbow off her upper arm, which was beginning to tingle, "that we do try to estimate the weight of experience in our lives."

"As if we can." He said this with a little snort that she found unaccountably piglike. He said it with disappointment.

"How else can we stand back and see where we are?" she said. "Or *who* we are?"

"Who we are." He echoed this observation lazily, without any fight in his voice or even a pull of breath. "You know that the 'who' of that particular question is something that absolutely cannot be isolated. Our identity shifts from one moment to the next, so that we are always in a state of becoming or diminishing."

Sandy set the "we" aside for the moment. As a historian, she believed obstinately in the roundness and accessibility of events. Every date had a doorway, if you could only locate it. Every recorded birth and death had its corporeal and metaphorical dust, composed or else scattered, the little lost frights and ecstasies of fragile existence. And there was something else that lived on top of her thoughts: the notion that everyone had a mother, and from that mother, from that tight little purse with its fleshy space and opening lips, came the desire for expanded air and space.

She felt the need to say so, even if it meant risking a non sequitur. "Each of us has had a mother," she murmured into Todd's neck.

"Yes," he said, but clearly without taking in the weight of her thought. "True enough."

"And yours?" she said, prodding.

"My what?"

"Your mother. You haven't mentioned your mother. Not so far anyway. Is she, you know, living?"

"Living, breathing. Housewife. San Diego. Arthritis in her fingers. Goes to Bible study. Cooks turkeys."

"Mine too. Amazing. All that same stuff. Only it's Danville, Ontario, not San Diego." She didn't tell Todd that she had put as much distance between herself and her mother as possible, or that she broke into a sweat when she heard her mother's voice on the telephone.

"My mother worries about beetles getting into her bread-box," Todd went on jovially.

"Really?"

"It's only happened once, in 1946, I think, before I was born, but it's given her a reason to stay alive."

"Has she read your book on seismic stasis?"

"Ha!"

"How reductive," Chloe said to Sandy, hearing about this conversation the next day. "Believing his mother's only worry is beetles in her bread. Her big worry is probably *him*. What a jerk she has for a son. Men who dismiss their mothers that easily can't be trusted."

"He said it rather sweetly, I thought."

"And I don't blame her one bit for not reading his book. Why the hell should she?"

"My mother read *my* book. She said I used too many big, show-off words."

"Really?"

"'Who do you think you are?'—that's what she said."

"If I were you, I'd wind this Todd thing up, and fast!"

"It's easy for you to say," Sandy told her. "You have Bernard. I haven't had anyone for a long time."

"Does he make you happy?"

"Happy?"

"Now, Sandy, that's a simple, straightforward question. Yes or no. Does he make your happiness gland wiggle and beg for more?"

"No. But."

———

It was summertime; Todd and Sandy were both free. He followed her back to Halifax and moved into the apartment she shared with her daughter. Just temporary, a few days. There was a heat wave. Then a cool wave. They spent a lot of time in bed—at least when Jenny was off at day camp. The rest of the day fell into a rhythm—reading the paper, cooking, shopping—that was comfortable, and that persuaded Sandy she was almost, in a summer kind of way, happy with her life.

At the same time, she had to admit that those twin demons, happiness and sadness, had lost their relevance. Happiness was a crock; no one, except maybe Chloe, really had it for more than a minute at a time. And sadness had shrunk, become miniaturized and narrowly defined, a syndrome, a pathology—whereas once, in another time, in a more exuberant century, in a more innocent age, there existed great gusts of oxygen inside the sadness of ordinary people, carpenters, tradesmen, housewives, and the like. Sadness was dignified; it was referred to as melancholy; it was described as autumnal in tone and tinged with woodsmoke. Nobody got blamed for the old sadness. It was a real affliction, like colour blindness or flat feet.

Matthew Hooke, for instance, could not be described as a happy man, and yet he was thought of as a valuable person in his society.

"Who actually is Matthew Hooke?" Todd had the courtesy to ask after a week or so.

"English botanist, 1809 to 1883."

"Yeah, right. The guy you wrote the book about."

"Uh-huh."

"Do you actually connect to this person? I mean, can he say to you anything that is actually meaningful? He's eighteenth-century—"

"Nineteenth-century." She had noticed that Todd was careless about dates.

"—and probably superstitious as hell and missing half his teeth. And here you are, this very twentieth-century woman who's lying in bed at three o'clock in the afternoon in a modern high-rise apartment in the middle of Halifax, and you haven't got any clothes on, just your skin against these sheets, and the traffic going by, and you turn your thoughts to this Hooke person—"

"Matthew Hooke."

"Right. Matthew."

"You sound jealous."

"What!"

"Jealous that I can be thinking of this mildly depressed but nevertheless intelligent and accomplished nineteenth-century gentleman at the same time you've got your hand between my legs."

"Well?"

"Well what?"

"Well, who's it going to be, then? Him or me?" He tried

to express this thought as a joke, but he was not, as Sandy had noticed, good at jokes.

"So." She attempted a playful tone. "Do I have to make a choice?"

"What, exactly, was so great about this man anyway? What's he done to get a biography written about him?"

"It's not a biography. It's more of a contextual mono-graph. A background inquiry into what made him who he was—"

"Whatever that was."

"I'm just a tiny bit surprised you don't know his work. Don't take this the wrong way, but, I mean, this was a man who paralleled Darwin, and whose ideas—"

"Look, I don't happen to be in that particular field. Who can know everything?"

"He did."

"He did what?"

"He was one of those late, late, late mediaeval polymaths who extended right into the nineteenth century. He knew science, literature, classical languages, philosophy, architec-ture, music. And botany—well, that goes without saying."

"The epistemological world was smaller then."

"You are jealous, aren't you?"

"It isn't as though he was Bach or Malthus or Kant or one of the great giants of human thought."

"He was an autodidact. A rustic from the wilds of Somerset. Never went to school."

"Oh, I get it. That's his excuse for being minor. He had hay coming out of his ears."

"Think of him as a synthesizer. That's how I describe him, anyway, in the book. Someone who skipped the heavy theoretical work and just talked about how plants looked, how they presented themselves. How they could change shape with a little encouragement."

"You don't need to be a genius to describe the various parts of a wood lily."

"Only a genius would think it's necessary to do so."

"What's that noise?"

"Oh God, it must be Jenny letting herself in the door."

"Jenny already?"

"Yes," Sandy said carefully, heavily. "Day camp is over for today. As it has been every day at this time. Children are put on the bus and brought home by their counsellors around about the middle of the afternoon. This happens all over the Western world."

"That's it, then, I suppose, for today."

She looked at him sternly, her schoolmarm look, and then let her face soften, pumping a theatrical puff of air into her cheeks. "There's always tomorrow."

Todd made a delicious macaroni-and-cheese supper for Sandy and Jenny, miles beyond the Kraft dinner they some-times shared on busy days. Rattrap cheese, tender pasta elbows, real grated onion, salt and pepper, all this baked slowly in cream until crisp. Ordinarily Sandy didn't keep cream in the house. This cream was left over from the veal recipe she'd cooked for Todd on the weekend.

"Can we eat in front of the TV?" Jenny asked.

"No."

"Why not?" The beginning of a whine.

"Because we should use the time to talk. You haven't told us what you did at day camp."

"We did a folk dance—I told you already. What Irish people do."

"That sounds very interesting," Todd said. "Some of those dances go back hundreds of years."

"Yes," Sandy said. "That's true."

"Courting dances," Todd said. "Or, more primitive still, dances that celebrate signs of fertility—the beginning of menses, for instance."

"So we did this folk dancing and then we did wood-work and then we had lunch and then we did birds and wildflowers and environment and then we waited for the bus to come."

"Well, maybe a little TV won't hurt. But only for half an hour."

"I know we agreed not to plunge into each other's history," Sandy said later to Todd, "and we've been pretty good about observing that pledge. But did you and your ex ever have children?"

"No," Todd said. "We thought about it a lot and we talked about it a lot. But it didn't happen."

"That's what I thought," Sandy said.

More and more, Sandy's men friends tended to be talky types, but perhaps they always had been. Her ex-husband, Jenny's father, Stephen, was a case in point: a man of bursting garrulousness, a physicist now employed at a research institute in Kansas City—thundering at his staff, no doubt, and filling the sedate laboratories with his galloping cadence. He was descended from a line of Missouri farmers who expressed themselves not sparingly, as country people are assumed to do, but colourfully, rapturously, endlessly, about crops, weather, and sports, and who exchanged the effervescent kind of quips that spin off from a more laconic tradition or else lean on common male assumptions: salesman jokes, penis jokes, beer jokes, jokes about city slickers or women's lib.

On the other hand, Stephen hadn't believed that every single issue under the sun warranted prolonged debate. The promotion of argument for its own sake sprang from a buried need for drama, according to Stephen. Talk should be a diversion, a pleasure, a pursuit, not something that spilled out of confession or declaration, so that the self was placed on trial. For instance, he, Stephen, did not plan to be in the labour room coaching Sandy when their baby was born. He wasn't at all frightened of the phenomenon, or repelled by it. He simply wasn't interested, period. Yes, he loved her and yes, yes, he would love the baby when it emerged, but he was not up to what he termed "the medical side of things."

His reluctance had seemed a big thing to Sandy at the time, a major betrayal that came to represent a number of other, smaller failings. Later she wondered why she had made such a big deal of it. Shouldn't she have appreciated the honesty of his response? "He's got a tongue on him," her mother had said, "but he won't ever bring you real trouble."

Later Sandy and her little Jenny lived for two years with a man named Christopher Swift, who sold computer stock. His was the kind of calling that demanded a quick phrase, a smooth delivery, a word-tumbling manner that forestalled interruption. The trouble was, he couldn't shut it off. He hovered over Sandy in the evenings, showered her with words on weekends, entertaining her, persuading her, pressing against her common sense, talking her into ridiculous ventures—a time-share in Hawaii, a hiking trip to Thailand, where Jenny nearly died of diarrhea and then dehydration.

There were others. Some lasted a matter of days. Mike Something-or-other and his philosophical divagations. He was a man who could turn a glimpse of an ordinary tree or shrub into an instant thesis on the insularity of the soul or hermeneutics of regeneration. Toby Shawn (six months) was given to meditations about his grandfather's incivility, his mother's spite, his brother's fecklessness—a circle of incrimination that widened endlessly and came to include, to no one's surprise, Sandy and eight-year-old Jenny. There was no refuge.

On lonely nights Sandy would head for the neighbourhood video store, where she rented old movies, particularly those from the forties, a time when her parents were children growing up. She would make a pot of tea, hunker down on a pile of cushions, and sit up half the night, eyes stuck to the screen, eager for the fiction of how men were once believed to behave.

She was particularly drawn to that American icon known as the strong, silent type, and a hopeful part of herself prompted her to believe that such men actually existed off the screen. Didn't Hollywood effusions, for all their carelessness, persist in the refining and sharpening of our vision of ourselves? That period creature the silent male did not babble or condemn or theorize or hold forth. He might open his mouth from time to time and speak when required, a dense, manly rumble in his throat introducing a terse, tender monologue of withheld energy, but he was not at any point bent crooked with the weight of his opinions. Instead his bone marrow quietly tapped into the world around him, the suppressed words subtly infantilizing his sexual bulk, so that you wanted to hug him like a baby and at the same time bed him down for a night of breathless, wordless, stunned satisfaction.

That was how it was in the old days, if you chose to believe it.

Sandy got a postcard from Chloe and Bernard, who were in Maine, stating, in Chloe's private cryptography, "Hope you're well out of the claws of Mr. Clause."

Everyone was surprised that Todd hung around right up until early September, when classes began at San Diego State, and that the usually impatient Sandy was not altogether exasperated by his presence. He fit in, more or less. He took Jenny to a dinosaur movie and out for pizza afterwards. His theory about the slippery self, its detachment from any fixed point of proof, had its own virtues, and even its comforts—at least for Sandy. Why should we be tethered to our inherited packet of DNA and to the tyranny of our mothers' and fathers' good intentions—what they might have done, what they could have said, if only they had been smarter, kinder, more feeling, less selfish? Does anyone apprehend human vibrations when they are filtered through choked time waves and genetic matter? How much can we know we know?

She had work to do at the end of the summer, lectures to prepare, her office to set in order. While she was out of the apartment, Todd busied himself reading about Matthew Hooke. He did this on the sly at first, working his way straight through Sandy's shelf of Hooke literature and then, finally, reading her book, *Matthew Hooke: Silent Visionary*.

He restrained himself, he later told Sandy, from making his usual marginal notations.

"What kind of notations would you have made?" She was surprised at how nervous she suddenly felt.

But all he said was, "Just the usual queries. Like 'Is this statement supported?' Or 'More information needed here.'"

She decided not to take this as a criticism. She decided to imitate the even-handed, non-judgmental woman she aspired to be. "Well, you've probably noticed that there isn't a lot of hard information about Hooke's life."

"Yes, I did notice."

"The only thing to do was to fill in around the edges with the historical background."

"Right."

She looked at him. "Eccentrics don't often leave complete records. They don't think they need to be forever explaining themselves."

In fact, his botanical journals aside, almost nothing was known of Matthew Hooke, nineteenth-century botanist, other than that he seldom spoke.

"Good day," he is believed to have said when presented to the Royal Court and honoured for his accomplishments in cross-breeding peas and, some years later, broad beans. He delivered his minimalist greeting, according to Sandy's text, not in the innocent manner of a rustic but in the full knowledge that his accomplishments released him from heavier forms of tribute or obeisance. He never married, never had children. He appeared to have lived without the consolation of sex—he who dabbled so happily, so tirelessly, with the tender male and female parts of plants.

Others who inhabited the same southwesterly English village as Matthew Hooke, a place called Little West Nutley, or sometimes simply West Nutley, knew him as a man of silence. Was he perhaps even simple, they might have wondered—a man so stretched by intensity and so out of joint with other human creatures that he misread the demands of common intercourse? The comments of his neighbours regarding his taciturnity were, of course, apocryphal, as was almost everything about poor Hooke's life: how he discovered his bent for natural science, how he overturned contemporary ideas of hybridization, how the tug of his thought moved ever towards the useful and practical, without losing for a minute the undertow of biological miracle.

"The kissing part took me by surprise," Todd told Sandy.

"Of course, we don't know quite how to read that aspect of his life," Sandy said. "I mean, we don't really know how weird or non-weird that kind of behaviour was."

"I'd say it was very, very weird," Todd said.

The kissing part was revealed in a single sentence inscribed by an unnamed West Nutley vicar who had undertaken to write a sort of village history. "Good Mister

Hooke speaks to no one excepting his pea blossoms," the vicar wrote, "but does love to kiss the ladies whenever an occasion is given."

"The guy was a pervert," Todd told Sandy. "A rapist manqué."

"I don't see it that way," Sandy said crossly.

"Leaping out of the bushes at ladies! Come on, now. Admit it."

"There's nothing in the text about leaping out of the bushes."

Sandy felt sure that Hooke's advances, if that's what they were, amounted to an innocent hunger for women's flesh—quick, dry kisses, aimed at the cheek or perhaps even the lips, shyly stolen, timid yet assertive, silent pressings, silken, a curious mouth seeking forbidden tenderness, requiring that fleet conjunction for its own sake and not for where such a kiss might lead or even what it might declare. A Hooke kiss would be enclosed by its own small muscular effort and release, and by the impossibility of an explanation outside the momentary refreshment that it offered. Its savour would break through the common parochial strictures like a new form of cloud and be permitted, even smiled over. Touch me, touch me, let me touch you in this simple, explicit way—that's all it would say. (Sandy had read somewhere that earthworms kiss, their frontal parts briefly waving, nodding at each other. Mosquitoes too, and houseflies, if the evidence could be believed. They caught each other in midair—a fraction of a second only, but a connection nevertheless.)

"You and your friend Chloe would have him up for sexual abuse if he wandered around Halifax stealing kisses."

"Maybe not. Maybe I'd like one of those stolen kisses myself. Maybe I'd feel honoured to be a recipient. Or maybe I'd think it was just, you know, sort of hilarious, but at the same time okay."

"So you believe that Matthew Hooke's personality was outside the margins. Psychologically speaking, I mean."

"Maybe. But not because he kissed ladies." She gave the word a cockney spin: *lie-dees.*

"What about his not talking?"

"I think I can understand that."

"Really! You! So you don't think he was even a little bit weird?"

"Well." She wanted to be fair. "There is that business about living with his mother."

"What business?"

"No particular business—just that he lived with her."

"Why shouldn't he live with her?"

"A grown man living with his mother. It's just—"

Sandy felt the conversation running out of control. She didn't know what it meant or who was defending whom, but she'd been here before often enough to understand how the most intricate arrangements can be dismantled by a single uttered phrase. Something hovered in the still air between Todd and her, a cloud of unbreathed thought, no bigger in size than a cantaloupe, or a human fist.

Then he said, "I live with my mother."

"Oh." Another skipped beat. "You didn't mention... I didn't realize."

"And I'll probably go on living with my mother."

"Oh."

"I didn't know it would matter to you. Or maybe I did know, and that's why I didn't bother to mention it."

"It doesn't mean a thing, not at all, really. You've completely misunderstood me, Todd. I have nothing against men who live with their mothers."

"Tell me about it." He said this as though his mouth were full of bitter coins.

This discussion took place on their last night together. For hours afterwards they lay silent on Sandy's bed, neither one of them really sleeping, and in the morning they rose to an even deeper silence, a silence she found painful but also dignified and somehow admirable. They moved politely around the apartment, two civilized adults, one of them preparing for an early flight, closing his suitcase, checking his ticket, attaching his E-mail address to the fridge with one of Sandy's rubberized fridge magnets. She made him toast and coffee, and then drove him, in silence, to the airport. The idea of an embrace seemed obscene. Shaking hands would have been ludicrous. All he said in parting was "Be sure to say good-bye to Jenny."

And give my love to your mother.

This is what Sandy told Chloe when they were having lunch a week later. "That's what I almost said to him— *Give my love to your mother.* The words were just about to hop off my tongue."

"What stopped you?"

"I don't know. I was afraid I might laugh. Or else cry. I mean, I'm a woman who doesn't know where her next kiss is coming from."

Eros

——

ANN WENT TO A party one night where the dinner
conversation drifted towards the subject of sexuality.
How does the sexual self get sparked into life? And when do
we suspect its shared presence?

The man sitting next to Ann at the table spoke author-
itatively on the subject. The sexual act, he said, requires a
verbal gloss these days. Other creatures—lesser creatures, he
meant—act out their sexuality instinctively, but human
beings have evolved to the point where they must second-
guess all natural feelings. A case of cultural over-refinement.
It can happen that people, so busy learning mathematics
or looking after their hair, simply don't "get it" on their
own, and then they need a sort of interpretive guide like
those types who take you on tours around hydraulic dams
or conduct wildflower walks. "These days explication is

required," he said, "in order to sanction the commands of the blood."

Ann disagreed with this man and said so. His name was Alex, and she'd been told he was a well-respected maker of mediaeval instruments with a studio in a converted warehouse not far from where she lives. She suspected he had been invited for her sake—it happened all the time, the well-intentioned matchmaking of her coupled friends. And so here they were, a single man, a divorced woman, the two of them seated next to each other, at the long, festive dinner table. Ann thought Alex's phrase "commands of the blood" was silly and old-fashioned, like certain kinds of poetry she remembered from school.

"Which is why," Alex continued, "we have had to develop the awful institution of the birds-and-bees talk between parents and children. Otherwise new generations could miss the whole thing, the mechanics, as it were, of what is required."

"That seems impossible," someone across the table said. "People don't grow to adulthood without knowing they're sexual animals."

Alex was adamant. He leaned his long arm forward so that the hairs on the back of his gesticulating hand were whitened by the twin circles of candlelight. "Individual children feel sexual urges, of course, but they don't necessarily know that other people do."

"You only have to turn on the TV—"

"And in prime time too!"

"—the new play at the Playhouse, I mean, talk about graphic—"

"Couldn't be more explicit."

"When I asked my mother about sex, she just wrung her hands and said, 'Don't you already know!'"

"More people than we think are locked in a circle of innocence," Alex said, nodding in a way that Ann thought was pretentious. "They resist. They block."

"All they have to do is read the newspaper."

"—spells out the whole whammy."

"—it doesn't quite, you know."

"Desire," said the woman whose dinner party it was. She stared deeply into her glass of red wine and said it again. "Desire."

The subject turned to Victorian brides who went to their marriage beds uninformed, how shocking that must have been, how perverse they must have found their husbands' expectations. *Now, my precious love, there is something I'm going to have to poke between your legs, but I promise to be gentle...*

"Maybe it did happen occasionally," Ann said, "but only someone terribly stupid could arrive at marriage age without adding up the perfectly obvious evidence all around them."

"You mean," someone said, "observing farm animals and the like?"

"Well, yes. And common everyday romance, which

has always been out in the open. Kissing, touching. Erotic glances. You have to know something's going on, that men and women have more happening between them than polite conversation and domestic convenience."

"Some people aren't particularly observant," Alex said, which suggested to Ann that he might be one of those people. "And some people aren't good at connecting the dots even when they see them."

A woman called Nancy Doyen mentioned a story she'd read in a newspaper. An Alabama couple had been married for a period of three years, at which time they visited a doctor, wondering why they had not been blessed with a baby. The doctor asked a few tactful questions, and soon established the fact that the couple had not had sexual relations. They had believed that sharing a bed—sleeping together— was all that was required.

"My point exactly!" Alex cried out. His voice was excited.

Ann gave him a long sideways look. He was the only man at the table who was not wearing a jacket and tie. Instead he wore a soft-looking woollen sweater in a deep shade of blue. Indigo, she supposed it would be called. The knit was particularly small and smooth for a man's sweater, and Ann reached forward and placed her hand lightly on the ribbing that formed the sweater's cuff. She had the idea that she must somehow restrain this person from making a fool of himself. He was looking into the candle-light with a Zenlike concentration, and Ann knew how, after a certain amount of wine, Zen talk leads straight to embarrassment.

He continued, though, her hand still resting on his wrist, to talk about the complicated notion of human sexuality, its secret nature and hidden surprises, its unlikelihood, in fact. As he talked he covered Ann's hand with his own, and then with one slow, almost absent-minded gesture he swept her hand into the shadows of his lap. She could feel the rough linen of the table napkin, then the abrupt soft corduroy of his trousers. She flexed her fingers, an involuntary movement, and a moment later found her hand resting against human flesh, the testicles laughably loose in their envelope of fine skin, and a penis, flaccid and small, curled up like a blind animal. Meat and two veg was how she and her girlfriends once described this part of the male body.

At first she thought she might laugh, and then she decided she might faint. She had never fainted in all her life, but this could be the moment. No one would blame her, especially those who knew about her recent surgery and chemo treatments.

Couldn't the others at the table hear the gasp gathering in her throat? She made a motion to pull her hand away from Alex's lap, but he pressed his fingers more firmly on hers. The thought came to her that these were the same fingers that constructed intricate lutes and lyres and handled small, probably beautiful tools. Her consciousness seemed to divide and to divide again, and then soften. She moved her fingers slightly, playfully, seeing what experiments she might invent. Even so small a movement had the effect of sucking the air out of the room, though no one seemed to notice.

"Desire," the hostess said once again. She probed her salad greens gently, then put down her fork and peered around the table of guests, a long visual arc of inquiry, of solicitude. Her wineglass was empty. Her look was loving and also proprietorial. She appeared pleased with every single one of them.

When Ann was four years old she was taken to stay for a few days with a married cousin who lived in the country. She has no idea how the arrangement came about. What could it have meant—a gesture of hospitality extended to a very young child? She does remember that she considered the visit a thrilling adventure.

Her cousin Sandra was a young woman, barely twenty, with a musical laugh and curls all over her head. She lived in a small brown house on an acre of land with her young husband, Gerald, and a tiny baby, Merry-Ann. There was about these arrangements the sense of a doll family afloat in a toy landscape, and this should have constituted a paradise for little Ann, whose own parents seemed immensely old and sombre and without movement in their lives.

She was allowed to push Merry-Ann in her carriage, first covering her with a crocheted blanket and tucking in the edges. She was permitted to stand on a kitchen chair and mash potatoes with Cousin Sandra's wooden masher. When Sandra and Gerald kissed, as they often did, Ann had the feeling of being inside the pages of a beautiful pop-up book with defined edges and dimensions and sudden, swallowed surprises and jokes.

Nevertheless, within a few days, three or four at the most, she grew anxious and miserable. She complained to her cousin of an earache, but the cousin identified the malady for what it was: severe homesickness. Her small suitcase was packed, and she was driven home.

She remembers that she was carried through the doorway of her own house—in whose arms she can never quite recall—and that she found the neutral, neglected rooms extraordinarily altered. In fact, only a few items had been changed. A leaf had been taken out of the breakfast table, and this smaller squarish table was now positioned at an angle under the window. Instead of the usual tan placemats there was a brightly flowered cloth, one Ann had never seen, and this too was placed at an angle. The scene was as jaunty and brave as a Rinso ad. Bright sunlight struck the edges of the plates and cups so that she had the sense of looking into a bowl of brilliant confetti, there were so many particles of colour dancing before her eyes.

This transformation had occurred in the short time she'd been away. It seemed impossible.

And even more impossible was the idea that her parents had been here all along. They had not been frozen in time or whisked out of sight. They had been alive, busily trans-forming the unalterable everyday surfaces, and here was the evidence. In her absence they had prevailed. They pos-sessed, it seemed clear, an existence of their own.

And there was something else that folded and filled the air. Something disturbing, vivid. It had no taste or noise to it, but it bulked in the space between her aproned mother and her father with his loosened necktie and rolled-up sleeves. "It" was a charged force, not that she could have described it as such, from which she herself was excluded, and it connected as through an underground passage with Cousin Sandra and Gerald kissing by the kitchen window, their mouths so teasing against each other, and yet so purposeful.

But that was all right. She liked it that way, and even if she didn't, she understood that this was the way things were and had, in fact, always been.

Yes, there was a thickening in the air, the spiked ether of unanswered questions.

But this was nothing new. Huge patches of mystery existed everywhere. How, for instance, to explain the halo around the head of baby Jesus? How did the voices get in-to the radio? That time when two neighbourhood dogs got stuck together: how could such an unlikely thing happen?

Ann, age seven, was caught at school holding a note that was being passed from desk to desk. The teacher, Miss Sellers, snatched it away and quickly scanned its contents. "I'm surprised at you, Ann," she said. "I'm very, very disappointed."

The note said: "Nelly, put your belly up to mine and wiggle your behind."

Ann was asked to stay in from recess until she had copied ten lines on a piece of paper: "I will not pass notes again." Later, deeply shamed and making her way out to the playground, she saw Miss Sellers in the stairwell. She was showing the note to two other teachers and they were laughing their heads off.

Aunt Alma and Uncle Ross came to visit every summer, and this visit was greatly anticipated, especially by Ann's mother. Aunt Alma was her favourite sister and the most beautiful. She wore daringly cut cotton dresses she made herself and was lively in her manner, spilling gossip and laughter. She knew how to "go at a tear," ripping through household tasks, the beds, the dishes, so that she and Ann's mother could head off for a day of shopping or out to lunch at a place called the Spinning Wheel. Sometimes, when Aunt Alma thought Ann was out of earshot, she told slightly off-colour jokes—but with a sense of wonderment in her voice, as though she herself with her elegant posture and thick coiled hair stood just outside the oxygen of these jokes, slightly bewildered rather than amused by the small, rough ironies of human bodies and the language that attended them.

Uncle Ross was tall, thin, and solemn. He spent the vacation days seated in a porch chair and going through a stack of *Reader's Digests* he'd brought along. There was no time to read during the working year, he explained; he was kept so busy at the insurance company.

One evening at the dinner table Uncle Ross paused before taking his place next to Aunt Alma. It happened to be a particularly hot day, and Aunt Alma was wearing a backless sundress. He bent and kissed the back of her neck, a slow and courtly kiss, unhurried, serious, and private— never mind that the whole family was present and about to dig into their roast beef hash.

This kissed part of Aunt Alma's neck was called the nape, which was something Ann didn't know at the time.

Ann, who must have been nine or ten years old, watched the kiss from across the table, and it seemed to her the kiss fell on her neck too, on that same shivery spot. She felt her whole body stiffen into a kind of pleasurable yawn that went on and on. So this was it. Now she knew.

Ann at fourteen spent hours at her desk practising an elegant backhand, which she believed would move her life forward. Her daily life was fuzzy, composed of what felt like carpet lint and dust, when what she wanted was clarity, poignancy. She memorized a love sonnet by Edna St. Vincent Millay, and she and her friend Lorna recited it in low moony tones, making fun of the words and of their own elocutionary efforts. She stared at the khaki pants of the boys in her class and wondered what was there, packed into the crotch and how it felt. Some boys she didn't know stopped her on her way home from school and poked a tree branch between her legs, which frightened her and puzzled her too, so that she broke away and ran all the way to her house. She cried at the movies; in fact, she liked only those movies that made her cry; her tears were beautiful to her, so clear, fast-flowing, and willing, yet so detached from the consciousness that she could watch them and mock them and snort at how foolish they were and how they betrayed her. At a New Year's Eve party a boy kissed her; it was part of a game, something he was obliged to do by the game's rules, but nevertheless she relived the moment at least once each day as though it were a piece of high drama, the softness of his lips and the giggling, eager embarrassment he'd shown. All these unsorted events accumulated in the same pocket of her brain, breathing with their own warm set of lungs. She read *Lady Chatterley's Lover*, and what shocked her most was that she found the book under a chair in her mother's bedroom.

Her mother knew; that was the terrible part. Her father knew too, he would have to know if her mother knew. Everyone knew this awful secret which was everywhere suggested but which for Ann lay, still, a quarter-inch out of reach. Even Bob Hope on the radio knew; you could tell by the way he talked about blondes and brunettes and red-heads. Oh, he knew.

———

"Don't ever let a boy touch your knee," Ann's mother told her. "It happened to me once when I was your age, but I knew that one thing could lead to another."

"A climax is like a sneeze," one of Ann's girlfriends said. "And you know how much everyone loves to sneeze."

"Boys love it if you put your finger in their ear. Not too hard, though. Just a tickle."

"The Tantric secrets," said an article Ann read in *Esquire* magazine, "can be easily mastered in a three-day course given on the shores of the beautiful Finger Lakes."

"I hope he never touched you," Ann's father said about a neighbour. "You'd tell us, wouldn't you, if he touched you."

High up on her inner thigh. That's where Ann touched herself. Making a little circle with her thumb.

"Sex and death. They live in the same breath, can't you feel that?" This from an English professor who detained Ann after class one day in order to discuss her essay on Byron.

"Be a nun and you get none," said an actress in a play Ann attended. The woman pronounced it loudly from centre stage, full of sly winks and meaningful shrugs.

"The body is a temple. Keep that temple sanctified for the man you are going to spend your life with. On the other hand, it's usually better if the man has had a little prior experience."

Molly Bloom. Yes, she said, yes, she said, yes. Something like that.

Ann married Benjamin. She had both her breasts in those days, and Benjamin adored those breasts. "You'd think they'd squeak when the nipple goes up," he said with wonder. He toyed with them, sucked them, gnawed gently at the tender breast skin, saying, "Grrrrr." The brown colour of the twin aureoles astonished him, though. He had expected pink, like in a painting. Ann wondered if the brownness frightened him slightly.

They had a wedding night, the kind of wedding night no one gets anymore. Before that night there had been long, luscious sessions of kissing, accompanied by a carefully programmed fumbling with each other's bodies: nothing below the waist, nothing under the clothes allowed, but nevertheless it was rapturous, those wet deep kisses and shy touches on her sweatered breasts.

Now here, suddenly, was Ann in a white silk nightgown with a lace yoke. Then the nightgown came quickly off, which seemed a shame considering its cost. Now his whole body was against hers; head to toe their warm young skin was in contact. This was the best part. The rest of the business hurt, and left a sticky, bloody puddle on the bedsheet, which worried Ann, how the hotel staff probably had to deal with such messes all the time.

She and Benjamin had read the marriage manual their

minister had given them, and in the chapter titled "Afterwards," the author had described a feeling of vague melancholy which often visits couples after a session of satisfying sex. There was a reason for this, something chemical, the hormones plunging to the baseline flatness of everyday life, a necessary return to the reality that sustains us.

And, yes, Ann remembered that wedding night plunge. Her whole body trembled with the sadness of it, and Benjamin, mistaking the trembling for orgasm, was proud, and then exhilarated, and then almost immediately ready to go again. Grrrrr, he said against her chest wall.

Things got better, of course. Then they got worse. Then they dramatically dwindled. There were violent quarrels in the early years that made Ann think of cloth tearing behind her eyes, and reconciliations so tender that even today her throat fills with tears when she recalls them. Sex was either a healing or an exercise in blame. Once she made the mistake of telling Benjamin that she found something faintly hilarious about sex, about how a man's penis suddenly blew up and wanted to stick itself in a woman's vagina; it was so ungainly, such a curious and clumsy human mechanism. He had taken this confidence badly. He liked to think of sex as a beautiful form of communion, he said, but Ann knows that he would not find her beautiful at this moment, with her battleground of a chest, that slicing breast scar and the curious new cords of hard tissue that join her shoulder and arm. Alex,

sitting next to her at a dinner table with her thumb and forefinger on his penis, will not find it beautiful either, never
mind the cheerful advice from the cancer booklets about the
return of the libido and new forms of touching and holding.

Benjamin's shame, his promises, his failures, his ardour,
his indecision—these formed the swampy terrain which
Ann learned more or less to navigate, understanding that
any minute the ground was likely to give way, but feeling
at the same time stronger, and more certain about what
she wanted. "I want you out," she finally said after one particularly bitter betrayal, and then, a week later, changed
her mind.

They went to Paris to patch things up.

Their hotel was located on a quiet street in the Marais
and faced onto a private park where Parisians walked their
dogs in the early mornings. Most of the other buildings
in the neighbourhood were built of a dull basement-
coloured stone, but the hotel where Ann and Benjamin
stayed was, rather curiously, constructed of a soft, rosy,
un-Parisian brick. Like many hotels, it wound its way
around a rectangular air shaft so that each room looked
directly into the windows of the other rooms. There was a
small garden at the bottom and a few lines of laundry, still
in the still air.

The hotel was classified as a luxury accommodation,
but it seemed during the week they were there to be undergoing a form of entropy. The air-conditioning failed. The

fax connection to the outside world failed. The extraordinarily heavy curtain on Ann and Benjamin's window fell to the floor, brass rod and all, and it took the two of them to carry it out to the corridor.

On the last day, after a breakfast of coffee and croissants, the elevator broke down. ("We do apologize, madame, but it is only five flights, just think of the guests on the top floors.") She and Benjamin climbed the stairs and entered their room. The faint and not unpleasant smell of cigar smoke greeted them, smoke that must have drifted across the air shaft from another room.

Benjamin lay on the bed, his eyes closed, and Ann settled in a chair by the open window, spreading her newspaper in front of her. She loved to read *Le Monde* when she came to France; its linguistic turns seemed a sort of crossword puzzle, and each time she managed to translate a sentence she congratulated herself.

Church bells rang out from a distance, reminding her that it was a Sunday morning. Traffic sounds rose from the street. A dog was barking, probably from the park across the street. Then she heard something else: a woman's strong orgasmic cry coming from one of the open windows of the hotel.

The innocence of it was what moved her first, the stunning lack of restraint. The music of the woman's moan was immediately recognizable to Ann, this half-singing, half-weeping, wordless release that seemed to block out all of

Paris, all of the hexagon of France with its borders and sea-coast and muted overhead sky.

Benjamin's eyes were suddenly open. He was smiling at her, and she was smiling back. Then they were out of their clothes—this happened in an instant—and into each other's arms. His skin felt exactly right to her that day, its silver flecks and familiar imperfections. As they moved together on the hard French bed the rhythm of their bodies took them over, in tune for once, and it seemed to Ann that the red bricks of their hotel were melting into a pool of sensuality. She had never understood that curious, over-weighted word *desire*, she had scoffed at that word, but this must be it, this force that funnelled through the open air, travelling through the porous masonry and entering her veins.

Everything, it seemed, could be forgiven and mended now. She imagined that each room on the air shaft was sim-ilarly transformed, that men and women were coming together ecstatically as she and Benjamin were doing and that the combined sounds they made formed an erotic random choir, whose luminous, unmoored music was spreading skyward over the city. This was all they ever needed for such perfect happiness, this exquisite permis-sion, a stranger's morning cry.

Of course it didn't last, how could it?

But she hangs on to the moment in these difficult days, even at this dinner table with her hand still in the lap of a

man named Alex, whom she hardly knows or even likes.
She is part of the blissful, awakened world, at least for a
moment. What comes in the next hour or the next year
scarcely matters.

Dressing Down

—

You MIGHT SAY THAT my grandfather carried the idea of "dressing down" to new heights.

He was, of course, a social activist of national reputation and, as well, the first serious nudist in southern Ontario, the founder of Club Soleil, which is still in existence, still thriving, on the shores of Lake Simcoe, just north of Toronto. You'll recognize his name at once if you're up on your twentieth-century history.

His biography came out too late—he had been dead for some years by then—for him to comment on or defend his own beliefs as a naturist, not that he would have done so, not that he would have entertained for two minutes the rude intervention of a press interview. *But how do you carry your wallet, sir? What do you do, sir, about, um, the male body's sudden embarrassments?*

Please, he would have said to the journalists from the *Toronto Star* or the *Globe* or the *Telegram* or whatever, please! The exposure of the skin to the sun and air is a private matter, and your interest in the project, gentlemen, ladies, is—forgive me—entirely prurient.

These same questions, I confess, also occurred to me as a young boy. How had my grandfather become a nudist in the first place and what did it mean to him to shuck off his clothes, all his clothes, for one month of the year? Was it so he could feel the gaze of a hot July afternoon spreading across the square lean acreage of his chest, and, in softer shadows, onto those other less talked about areas? And, another question, how did he reconcile his nudist yearnings with his Wesleyan calling, with his eleven-months-a-year job as YMCA director for Eastern Canada?

If you drive the highway to Lake Simcoe today, you'll be struck by the variety of signs greeting you left and right between the groves of pine and birch: one by one they gesture towards green-leafed darkness, offering winding trails, gravel roads, pointing the way to countless small hidden lakes, beaches, and stretches of inspirational shore. "Awake-Again Bible Conference." "Bide-a-Wee Housekeeping Cottages, Reasonable Rates.". "The Merit Institute. Absolutely Private." "Fish 'n' Fun with Mike and Hank." "STOP AND SAY HELLO—TED AND TINA." "ADX Yoga and More." And, finally, "Club Soleil."

Club Soleil has never, not since its founding in 1926,

had more than the most discreet of highway signs, hand-painted, black on white, a single board nailed to the trunk of a long-lived elm, with a roughly fashioned arrow-tip pointing east towards a trail, one that discouraged (yet allowed) wheeled traffic.

Campers at Club Soleil slept in tents in the early years. Meals, vegetarian, were taken beneath the shade of an immense canvas structure known as The Meeting Place. Why vegetarian? Why Carrot Soufflé on Monday, Parsnip Purée on Tuesday, Swiss Chard Pie on Wednesday, and so on and so on? My grandfather was a meat eater for the rest of the year, but in July he lived on leaves, roots, seeds, the only nourishment going at Club Soleil.

The prohibition against the eating of flesh might seem to some visitors a contradiction when human flesh was every-where displayed on the Club Soleil lawns and on the narrow strip of beach running around a promontory called The Point. The living hams and haunches of middle-aged men made their way between mixed flower and vegetable beds, another of my grandfather's innovations. And so did the necks, shoulders, throats, and bellies of their wives. White-jellied breast flesh jiggled in the Ontario sunlight, tested it, defied it. Buttocks. Thighs. Calves. Fragile ankle bones be-longing to city lawyers, physicians, charity organizers, house-hold matriarchs. Patrician feet stepped carefully across the beach pebbles and drummed up and down on the grass where a volleyball court had been set up for the young people.

My grandmother had difficulty with all this. It was only after she and my grandfather were married that he told her how he had been taken by friends soon after finishing university to a naturist beach on the Atlantic coast of France. He had greeted the new experience as a door swinging wide open in his existence. Some men are brought to life by the sexual spasm; my grandfather tasted ecstasy for the first time as he lowered his trousers on the slope of a French sand-dune, then, more cautiously, dropping his underwear as well, then stepping free. Dry heat and sunlight penetrated his dark manly parts, which since birth had been confined. A hundred other bathers looked on, or rather, they *didn't* look on, that was the wonder of it, that they never so much as glanced in his direction.

He had not expected in his life to feel a breeze pass over his nether regions—this is the untethering miracle he tried to explain to my grandmother, and later to her son, my father. The pleasure was intense and yet subtle. It resonated across the width of his skin, the entire human envelope electrified—here was paradise. And it was in accord with nature's design, as he saw it. It was true; he was able to see nothing perverse about his reaction. How could it be so when he became at that pants-dropping moment larger, stronger, nobler, a man charged with a new range of moral duty? The Protestant God of shame had nodded in response, nodded and smiled and drifted away, and my grandfather, so unexpectedly twitched into life, announced himself an instant convert. He walked straight into the sea, then, where the cold salt water flowed around every mound and recess of his body and completed the arc of liberation.

But how was he to bring the same set of circumstances and appreciations to rigid Ontario? And how, a year later, to explain his passion to his young bride, my gently brought-up grandmother?

He was a man, however, who took for granted his right to make his dreams come true. Ever methodical in his dealings, he sent away to the International Naturism Institute in Switzerland for information, then began to look for a piece of well-sheltered lake property which he was able to purchase with part of his inheritance. Next, he carefully sounded out a few of his more worldly friends. Might they be interested? Had they discovered for themselves the health-giving benefits of naturism, psychological as well as physical, the mind and body unfettered and fused? Did they know of others who might be interested in the venture? Discretion would rule the day, of course. Privacy, sanctuary, a quiet bond between comrades, an agreement to give one's self up to the pleasures that God Himself had provided.

Yes, my grandmother said, but this is not the sort of thing that remains secret, no matter how circumspect one is.

She was right. Word got around. It was inevitable. But

her husband's passion for health and sun, his annual indul-
gence, only enhanced his dignity. It seemed he could do
no wrong in those days. The imagined presence of this
young, muscular, unclothed body, released to nature, to
prelapsarian abandonment, and its contrast to the suited,
shirted, necktied manliness he presented to the world as
he went about lecturing on social justice or presiding over
his YMCA duties—this misalignment only gave him a
beguiling, eccentric edge, arousing even in the strait-laced
a shrugging admiration and making of him an exceptional
being, free-minded, liberal, a man of virility, who also
happened to be clever and compelling—especially to
women. He became, in the puritanical society he inhabited, rather famous.

My grandmother's disinclination for nudity would not have
surprised those who knew her well. Her interest was in covering up, not stripping down. The same week she married
my grandfather she'd had curtains and heavy draperies made
for the windows of the house they bought on Macklin
Avenue. By the following summer slip-covers dressed the
wicker porch furniture. Scarves in broderie anglaise adorned
every bureau. Pillows in my grandparents' house were fitted
with under-covers as well as over-covers, and she herself
sewed a sort of skirt in flowered chintz, which was tied pret-
tily with bias tape around the wringer washing machine
when it was not in use. Lace doilies sat on the arms and back

of every chair. Woollen throws were flung across the various sofas. Rugs lay scattered everywhere upon the thick carpets. Fullness, plumpness, doubleness. Hers was a house where one could imagine the possibility of suffocation.

Her own clothing, needless to say, comprised layers of underclothes, foundation garments, garters and stockings, brassieres, camisoles, slips, blouses, cardigans, lined skirts, aprons, and even good aprons worn over the everyday aprons. Her mind drifted towards texture, fabric, protection, and warmth, as though she could never burrow deeply enough into the folds of herself.

Which was why she had so much difficulty taking part in the annual July rites at Lake Simcoe. Naturism was not her nature. Nudity was the cross she bore.

At first she tried to make bargains with her husband. "I'll go," she told him, "but don't expect me to go around with *my* clothes off."

He reasoned with her gently, reminding her that nudity was an activity that, once established, did not allow abstentions. Nudity implied community. The effort to throw off cultural ignorance was so difficult, he explained, that reinforcement was ever needed. A single clothed person creates a rebuke to the unclothed. One person walking across the Club Soleil lawn in a summer dress and sandals and underpants is enough to unsettle others in the matter of the choice they had taken.

But going without clothes was unhygienic, she argued.

No, he said, not at all. (He had read his material from the International Naturism Institute closely.) Woven cloth harbours mites, moulds, dust, germs. Whereas nothing is easier to keep clean than human skin, which is, in fact, self-cleaning.

Infection, my grandmother pointed out. From others.

Not a chance, he argued. Not when every camper is issued a clean towel at the beginning of the day, and this towel is used on the various benches and hammocks at Club Soleil, and even carried into the dining hall and spread on the chair before the diner sits down.

"It's different for women," she protested, gesturing awkwardly, miserably. "Women have special problems."

My grandfather explained that when women campers were 'having their time," they had only to wear a short pleated skirt, rather like a tennis skirt. No one thought a thing of it, six days, seven days, nature's timetable. There was, of course, no reason to cover the breasts or shoulders.

"I can't imagine Mrs. Archie Hammond going around naked, not with her sags and bags." My grandmother said this with uncharacteristic bitterness.

"Kate and Archie have both signed up."

"Naked? Those two?"

"Of course, naked. Though naked, my love, is not really a word that naturists use."

"Yes, you've told me. A hundred times. But naked is naked."

"Semantics." (My grandfather, it must be remembered, lived in the day when to snort out the word *semantics* was enough to win any quarrel.)

"You do know what people will say, don't you?"

"Of course I know. They'll say that visitors to Camp Soleil are licentious. That we are seekers of sexual pleasure, and that the removal of the artificial barrier of clothing will only inflame our lust. But these people will be wrong."

"I'm not so sure of that," she said. "I know Archie Hammond. I've seen how he looks at women, even with their clothes on."

"Our bodies are God's gifts. There are those who believe that our bodies are holy temples."

"Then why," she asked cannily, "don't you ever see pictures of Jesus without *his* clothes on? He's always got that big brown robe wrapped around him. Even on the cross he had a little piece of cloth—"

"This discussion is going nowhere."

Indeed this discussion would have gone nowhere. It would have vanished into historical silence, except that my grandfather confided its essence to his adult son— my own father—years later, where it was received, as such parental offerings are, with huge embarrassment and rejection. How could such a private argument have taken place between one's own mother and father? Why this mention of the unmentionables between them, infidelities, monthlies—was it really necessary?

"Don't you see," my grandmother, not yet thirty years old, said to her husband, "how humiliating this is for me? A grown-up woman. Playing Adam and Eve at the beach."

He was touched by the Adam and Eve reference. It brought a smile to his lips, threw him off course. This was not what she intended.

"Do it for me," he pleaded. He had a slow, rich, persuasive way of speaking. "Please just try it for me."

"Would you love me less if I refused?"

"No," he replied. But he had let slip a small pause before he spoke, and this was registered on my grandmother's consciousness.

"It's wrong, you know it's wrong. It fans those instincts of ours that belong to, well..."

"To what? Say it."

"To barnyard animals."

"Ah!"

"I can't help it. That's what I think."

"We are animals, my precious love."

"You know what I mean."

"Why don't we make a bargain, then?"

She was suspicious of bargains. She came from a wealthy Ontario family (cheese, walnuts, whisky) where bad bargains had been made between brother and sister, father and son. "What kind of bargain?" she asked.

"You're crying."

"I have to know. I need to know."

"I propose that during the month of July we abstain."

"Abstain?"

"From sexual intercourse."

"But"—she must have paused at this point, hating this term *sexual intercourse*, and yet shocked that her husband would relinquish so easily their greatest personal pleasure— "why?"

"To prove to you, conclusively, that going unclothed among those we trust has nothing to do with the desires of the flesh."

"I see."

My grandmother was a passionate woman, but probably shy about the verbal expression of passion—and not sure how to show her shocked disappointment in the proposed accommodation. "I don't know what to think," she said, tears lining her lashes, knowing she had somehow been trapped in her own objections.

And so she was now faced with a dilemma. Her husband had countered each of her arguments about Club Soleil, and had even offered the ultimate sacrifice, an abstention from intimate relations during the unclothed month of July. She was cornered. She must respond, somehow, and of course she was at an age when people believe they will become more and not less than they are.

"All right," she said to the proposed bargain. "All right."

Did she say it crossly or tenderly? With a sense of defeat or victory? The particular tone of the story has not come down to me.

And so the long succession of summers began, the humiliation of July first when my grandmother's favourite flowered dresses came off, her girdle, her hose, her underpants. There is a certain sharp irony to be felt when cast in a role one can't quite occupy, and for my grandmother a jolt of anger must surely have accompanied her acquiescence, the beginning of a longer anger. She found a way to walk on the beach with reasonable dignity, but never with ease, and she learned to stand nodding and chatting with Kate Hammond and the other women, blocking out the sight of their bared, softening flesh, discussing the weather, the children, the latest movies and books. She never, apparently, became accustomed to her exposed body with its pale protrusions, its slopes and meadows and damp cavities. Her fair face lightly perspired in the fresh breeze. Always she carried herself with an air of dolefulness, her eyes wary, her hands crossed stiffly over the region of her pubis. Stiff with love and suffering and absence.

This went on for years. My grandparents and the other original members grew older. Some of them retired and moved to Florida, but a new and younger set of naturists joined the ranks. Archie Hammond died of a heart attack, though Kate Hammond remained a loyal summer camper, moving from a tent into one of the newer cabins. The tennis courts were upgraded. A vegetarian chef was brought from Banff.

Then, suddenly one summer, my grandmother refused to take part. The cause of her refusal was me, her ten-year-old grandson, who was to be taken to Club Soleil for the first time. It was one thing, she felt, to take off her clothes in front of her husband and friends; she had hardened herself to the shame of it. But she would not become a naked grandmother, she would not allow herself to surrender to this ultimate indignity. This was asking too much.

She remained in Toronto that summer, and the rupture between herself and my grandfather was never completely mended.

It might be wondered why I was not introduced to Club Soleil until I was ten years old. I loved my grandparents, and had often wondered where they disappeared to each summer. I sensed some reticence, distaste even, on my father's part when it came to discussing the matter. *Soleil* was a French word, he explained carefully, meaning sunshine. Our own vacations—my mother, father, and I, their only child—were taken at Muskoka Lodge, where the wearing of clothes was unquestioned, and indeed may have been part of the reason for going there. It was a fashionable place in those days, and a full wardrobe of "resort apparel" was de rigueur. I remember that my mother possessed a pale peach dress with a little "bolero" that floated behind her as she stood leaning on the porch rail during the evening cocktail hour. My father, of course, ended each day by exchanging his golf clothes for a white dinner jacket.

Then one year they decided to go to Europe instead, and someone suggested that I should stay behind and join my grandparents at Club Soleil. The idea of perpetual *soleil* was appealing, especially since our own Muskoka Lodge summers were often cloudy or rain-soaked.

At this point the real nature of the enterprise was explained to me, and I remember my father's words as he struggled to fill me in. "It is a place," he said, "where people go about in their birthday suits."

I knew what birthday suits meant. It was one of the jokes of the schoolyard. Birthday suits meant buck-naked, stark-naked. Starkers.

"You mean with nothing on?" I was deeply shocked, though I later wondered if part of my shock was rehearsed and just slightly augmented for effect.

My father coughed slightly. "It's believed, you see, to be good for the health. Vitamin D, the sunshine vitamin."

"Not even their swimsuits?" This came out in a theatrical squeal. It seemed important to reach a full understanding at once, to get it over with.

"I know it's difficult to imagine." He patted me on the shoulder then, a rare gesture from a man who lacked any real sense of physical warmth.

Oddly, the thought of my grandmother's naked body lay well within my powers of imagination. I had inspected the plump nylon-encased feet and legs of my mother, so rosy, sleek, and unscented, and I'd also seen the statues in the park and at the art gallery, the smooth marble parts of women, unblemished and still and lacking human orifices. What shocked me far more was thinking of my unclothed grandfather, a man who had always seemed to me *more* clothed than other men. His dark business suits were thicker of fabric and more closely woven. And there were his tight collars, black hose, serious oxfords, and the silk scarf he tucked in the neck of his woollen overcoat so that not an inch of flesh, except for his hands and face, was available for scrutiny. But this was my winter grandfather, the only one I had ever seen. Could he possibly have, tucked between his trousered legs, what my father had, what I had?

Yes, it turned out that he did, but instead of hiding these parts behind a bath towel as I was taught to do at home, he strolled the grounds of Club Soleil, an elegant man at home in his own aging, pickled-in-brine skin, a revered ascetic and—it was clear—lord of his own domain, majestic in his entitlement, patting the heads of children and stopping to chat with Kate Hammond at the edge of the archery range. "You must not be afraid," he said to me kindly on the day of my arrival, "to follow the rituals we observe in our summer community."

To be encouraged in such sanctified naughtiness was beyond any dream a ten-year-old boy might have. I learned. I learned fast, but at the same time I understood that the world was subtly spoiled. People with their limbs and creases and folds were more alike than I thought. Skin tones, hairy patches; that was all they had. Take off your clothes and you were left with your dull suit of invisibility.

What I witnessed led me into a distress I couldn't account for or explain, but which involved a feverish disowning of my own naked body and a frantic plummeting into willed blindness. I was launched into the long business of shame, accumulating the mingled secrets of disgust and longing, that eventually formed a kind of rattling carapace that restricted natural movement and ease.

"I'm only sorry," my grandfather said often that summer, "that your grandmother is not here to see how brown and strong you've grown."

When my grandfather died he was buried in a plain pine coffin, just as the instructions in his will outlined.

And his tall and by now greatly withered body was laid out on the bare floor of the coffin without a stitch to conceal his nakedness and not even a blanket or sheet for comfort's sake. This was not his request, but my grand-

mother's, grimly decreed when the family gathered to discuss the "arrangements." She insisted it would have been
what he wanted, and since the coffin was to be closed, what
difference did it make. She also insisted that Mrs. Kate
Hammond be barred from the funeral.

"It is impossible to bar anyone from a public funeral,"
my father insisted.

"Then she is not to be invited to stay for coffee afterwards," my grandmother said. "She will probably come
anyway, but she is not to be explicitly invited." She said
this sternly, punitively it seemed to her family, in an
attempt to outflank her dead husband, but by then all of
us had learned to shrink from the anger that deformed her
last years.

Her own death, pneumonia, occurred a mere eighteen
months after my grandfather's. She too had specified in her
will a plain pine box, with the additional written request
that her body be put to rest unclothed and that the coffin
be left open at the funeral.

It was as though she had hungered for this lewd indis-
cretion, as though some large smouldering ugliness had
offered itself to her in her last days and she had been unable
to resist. That's what I thought at the time.

Now I think of that final gesture differently. (Needless
to say, the family did *not* honour her final request, the pine
coffin, yes, and yes to the naked body, but the lid was firmly
closed.) It seems to me now that an offering was made on

her part, heartbreaking in its impropriety and wish for amends. This desire perhaps had acquired a grotesque life of its own, with a vividness that could find no form of expression in the scannable universe. "The unclothed body," she might have said, pouring into that vessel of a word a metaphorical cleansing, "is all we're allowed to take away with us."

The rest must have fallen away in the same moment she wrote down the words of her will: the draperies, the coverings, the fringe and feathers, the wrappings, the linings, the stuffings and stitching. Good-bye, she must have said to what couldn't be helped. Good-bye to the circular life of shame and its infinite regress.

She must have thought she could get everything back by a single act of acquiescence. In the next world, just a breath away, the two of them would greet each other rapturously. Their revealed limbs would flash among the bright vegetation, at home in the green-clothed world, and embracing each other without restraint.

She would have forgotten that nature's substance is gnarled and knotted in its grain, so that no absolutely straight thing can come of it. They should have understood that all along, those two. It might have become one of their perishable secrets, part of the bliss they would one day gladly surrender.